Cover Copy

Falling for her isn't permitted.

Following the brutal murder of his father and elder brother, James Hargrove, the Earl of Donnelly, comes into a title he never expected. His future was set, to join the 18th Royal Hussars and dedicate his life to his king and country. Now, he's been dragged into the shadowy depths of the underworld as he seeks to discover the impossible—to uncover who murdered his loved ones.

Lady Sophia Trentbury has long since loved the earl and fears for his life when she learns of his decision to uncover who murdered his father and brother. She'll do whatever it takes to aid him in his mission, even if she must immerse herself in London's deadly underworld of spies and espionage.

As the earl is swept into a lethal circle of deadly enemies, he must discover what is truth and what is deception, and all while protecting the scorching love of his lady who won't leave his side, even when he demands it. Can he hope for victory?

Books by Joanne Wadsworth

The Matheson Brothers Series
Highlander's Desire, Book One
Highlander's Passion, Book Two
Highlander's Seduction, Book Three
Highlander's Kiss, Book Four
Highlander's Heart, Book Five
Highlander's Sword, Book Six
Highlander's Bride, Book Seven
Highlander's Caress, Book Eight
Highlander's Touch, Book Nine
Highlander's Shifter, Book Ten
Highlander's Claim, Book Eleven
Highlander's Courage, Book Twelve
Highlander's Mermaid, Book Thirteen

Regency Brides Series
The Duke's Bride, Book One
The Earl's Bride, Book Two
The Wartime Bride, Book Three
The Earl's Secret Bride, Book Four
The Prince's Bride, Book Five
Her Pirate Prince, Book Six
Chased by the Corsair, Book Seven

Books by Joanne Wadsworth

Highlander Heat Series
Highlander's Castle, Book One
Highlander's Magic, Book Two
Highlander's Charm, Book Three
Highlander's Guardian, Book Four
Highlander's Faerie, Book Five
Highlander's Champion, Book Six
Highlander's Captive (Short Story)

Princesses of Myth Series
Protector, Book One
Warrior, Book Two
Hunter (Short Story - Included in Warrior, Book Two)
Enchanter, Book Three
Healer, Book Four
Chaser, Book Five

Billionaire Bodyguards Series
Billionaire Bodyguard Attraction, Book One
Billionaire Bodyguard Boss, Book Two
Billionaire Bodyguard Fling, Book Three

The Earl's Bride

Regency Brides, Book Two

JOANNE WADSWORTH

The Earl's Bride
ISBN-13: 978-1-97350-282-1
Copyright © 2017, Joanne Wadsworth
Cover Art by Joanne Wadsworth
First electronic publication: December 2017

Joanne Wadsworth
http://www.joannewadsworth.com

AUTHOR'S NOTE:
This book is a work of fiction. The names, characters, places, and incidents are products of the writer's imagination or have been used fictitiously and are not to be construed as real. Any resemblance to persons, living or dead, actual events, locale or organizations is entirely coincidental. The author does not have any control over and does not assume any responsibility for third-party websites or their content.

Published in the United States of America

First digital publication: December 2017
First print publication: December 2017

Chapter 1

Donnelly House, London, 1810.

"I must uncover who murdered my father and brother." James Hargrove, the Earl of Donnelly, leaned back in his study chair, his head resting against the high supporting headrest. Grief clung to him, so dark and dismal and never ending since the death of his beloved family members. "They would expect no less of me."

"Yes, but uncovering who murdered them has presented a challenge thus far." The Duke of Ashten stood at James's study window, his hands clasped behind his back and shoulders stiff as he cast his gaze over the rear gardens, the late afternoon light of the day shimmering through the trees and dappling the grass. With one brow quirked, his friend cast him a glance over his shoulder. "Think on it, Donnelly. The Bow Street runner has concluded his investigations and reported that their deaths were accidental. It will be a challenge to convince anyone else of it otherwise."

"There is nothing accidental about their drowning, not

when they were both exceptional swimmers." He thumped one fist on his desktop. "They perished three nights apart, their bodies pulled from the same stretch of the River Thames alongside my father's warehouses."

"Yes, I agree that's far too coincidental, and I believe as you do, that there is a killer on the loose. Unfortunately, it's been so long. Two months have passed since they perished, and no new information has come to light."

"Foul play was most certainly involved." He wouldn't relent on that, the knowledge burning deep in his gut.

"George was grief stricken following your father's death." Ashten crossed his arms, his brow wrinkling. "When I visited him here at Donnelly House, he'd consumed an entire decanter of brandy and was barely in full command of his senses."

"My brother would never have left Maria behind. Our sister needed him."

"I instructed your butler to put him to bed, then ensured your sister slept." Ashten gestured to the pile of papers on his desk. "Have you sifted through all of your father's papers yet? Our greatest chance of finding any reference to foul play will either be here, or at his warehouse office."

Donnelly had only been home a week, his journey back across the English Channel a difficult one since he'd been on the move with his fellow hussars at the time of receiving word of his father and brother's deaths. It had taken time to extricate himself from their front-line location and make his way back to England's shores.

"I've investigated each and every one of my father's business dealings and there isn't anything either he or my brother didn't handle with absolute professionalism, even with regard to the sunken treasure you and I have already spoken about. Although it is that treasure which still irks me the most, particularly since it went missing from the War Office where my father and brother had it sent to."

Over the past few years, his father had invested heavily in his maritime trade ventures, his brother standing firmly at his father's side, those ventures exceedingly lucrative. For certain the dealings they'd undertaken had increased their Donnelly wealth to the point where their coffers overflowed with coin.

"I will fully search his warehouse office in the morning. Would you be free to offer your aid? An extra set of eyes is always helpful," he asked Ashten.

"Certainly. Collect me from Blackgale House in the morning." Firm agreement.

"Thank you."

"Have you had luck contacting the man I gave you the name of?" Ashten crossed to him and pressed his palms against the polished oak desk, the sleeves of his superfine navy jacket rising and exposing the gold cufflinks adorning his pristine white shirt.

"Yes, I've managed to track Captain Anteros Bourbon down. The spymaster is elusive and prefers keeping to the shadows, but I located him at a gaming hell, his own establishment as I came to learn—*The Cobra*. Or I should say he located me while I was searching for him." Captain Bourbon certainly held a complex network of connections that reached into the dark depths of the underworld, a network he hoped would aid him in uncovering the truth about what had happened to his father and brother. No matter that the Bow Street runner had concluded their deaths were accidental, they'd been killed, and he was certain of it.

"Bourbon will uncover anything that reeks of foul play." A reassuring nod from Ashten. "I give you my word he will."

"After I gave him all the information I held, he told me he'd be in touch. He certainly seemed interested in my case when I spoke of the sunken treasure and its disappearance."

"Yes, Bourbon enjoys a challenge, and your case will surely provide it. That sunken treasure is the key, I believe." Ashten returned to the window and grasped the sill, his gaze alert.

"No harm will come to your wife and her sister outside." Donnelly stood and joined his friend and comrade. Along the stone pathway lined with white and pink flowering bushes, Ashten's new bride and her sister strolled, their golden-haired heads bent close together. When his butler had announced the duke's arrival, along with the two ladies who'd traveled with him, he'd asked Woodman to show Ashten to his study, and to ensure the ladies made themselves at home. They'd chosen to enjoy a stroll outside while he conversed with Ashten, which suited him well, particularly since he didn't wish to speak to Ashten's new sister-in-law, Lady Sophia Trentbury. Only trouble lay down that pathway if he did.

"Sophia's been quite worried about you." Ashten quirked a brow. "I realize things didn't end well between the two of you when you chose—on the day you rode out with the hussars no less—to end your courtship fully and finally. You're an idiot for letting her go, Donnelly, a true imbecile." An exasperated shake of the duke's head. "A dolt through and through. Of the greatest sort. In case you haven't quite got my meaning yet. Shall I go on?"

"I understand perfectly." It had nearly ripped his heart in two to set Sophia free, but better that than to ask her to wait until he returned home from the war, if he ever did. So many good men had perished in their battle against Napoleon, and so many more still would to come. This war of atrocity loomed endlessly over all of Europe.

"You told Sophia to enjoy what remained of the Season, that you wished her well. She was both furious and heartbroken, although even worse, you've turned her away each time she attempted to visit you and your sister this past week. She had been calling by and keeping Maria company until you returned, and doing a fine job at it too. You're a cad and a coward."

"Good grief, old chap. Lay it out." He slapped Ashten on the back. "Don't hold back."

"I won't." A smile tugged at Ashten's lips. "You're rather hard to stay angry with at times."

"My father used to tell me the same, and I had to be abrupt with Sophia, otherwise she would have waited for my return, for years if need be." No matter his return, he still couldn't pick up with his sweet Sophia where he'd left off. A murderer remained on the loose, a killer possibly intent on coming for him next, and whether that was an absolute possibility or not, he'd rather take his own life than allow Sophia's to be stolen from her because he had selfishly wanted to keep her for himself. "Until I know who killed them, and why, I can't commit myself to another woman."

"I understand, but Sophia is so very much like my Ellie." Ashten sat on the edge of the sill, his arms crossed and sunlight streaming over his jacketed shoulders. "Both sisters hold those they consider family close to their hearts, and Sophia has always considered you and Maria family, no matter your broken courtship. When she asked if she could ride with me to see you today, I, of course, agreed."

"My butler did inform me of Sophia's visits with Maria while I was across the channel, but they can't continue now I'm home. She'd be entering the home of a single gentleman, which even Winterly should be standing up and disallowing." Sophia's brother, the Earl of Winterly, was a man he considered a friend and confidant, a man who needed to consider his sister's safety above all else. Safety which didn't exist around him, not with all surety.

"Maria is her friend, and Sophia brought her maid with her while you were away, a guard too. She was well chaperoned. Where is Maria, by the way?" A huff as Ashten asked that. "You haven't locked her away in her bedchamber, have you?"

"Of course not. Maria's resting. She didn't sleep well last night." He glanced out the window and followed Sophia's footsteps as she wandered the pathways of his rear gardens. Like an elixir to his senses, he wanted to drown in the returned sight of her. Her rose-colored day gown accentuated her slim waist and flared over her hips, the dainty capped sleeves framing her creamy shoulders, while her golden curls swept down her back underneath her matching silk bonnet. When she bent to smell the fragrant blooms of the yellow roses, that bush in particular having been his mother's favorite, the scalloped neckline of her gown dipped forward, and he received a rather alluring view of her lush breasts.

Such incredible torture.

She wound one loose golden curl around her finger, and he groaned.

A sudden lift of her head, and she snagged his gaze.

He jerked back.

No eye contact.

Too dangerous.

Clearing his throat, he returned to his desk and plunked into his chair. "One very fortunate man will make Sophia an offer of marriage, and she'll become the wife of another, which I have resigned myself to. Things simply can't return to the way they were considering my treatment of her. She must detest the sight of me."

"You are underestimating her." Ashten *tut-tutted* under his breath, then opened the window a notch wider and smiled down at the ladies. "Are you two enjoying your walk?"

"Yes, very much." Sophia's heavenly voice floated through the window opening, both a balm to his senses and a searing danger as well. "Donnelly, I know you're there and currently ignoring me. May I speak with you, please?"

"Lord Donnelly?" Ashten eyed him expectantly. "I believe Lady Sophia is trying to gain your attention."

"I'm busy." Rocking back in his chair, he made sure to say that nice and loud, so Sophia wouldn't miss his answer through the window.

"Unfortunately," Ashten said with a ragged sigh to Sophia, "the earl is unable to converse with even a modicum of politeness at present. You'll have to excuse his terribly obnoxious behavior and count yourself lucky you're not in here with me."

"I'm coming upstairs this instant. Obnoxious behavior included." An exasperated huff. "Inform the earl."

"We'll see you momentarily." With a distinct smirk, Ashten closed the window and leaned one shoulder against the window frame. "I admire her determination."

"You would." He wanted to toss Ashten out his window.

Footsteps thumped up the stairs and his study door swung open.

Sophia stood in the doorway, her piercing blue gaze locked on him and fire blazing within their passionate depths. "Unable to converse, my foot."

"I am extremely busy." He motioned to the pile of papers.

"I will not accept that answer, and why have you forbidden my entrance into your house this past week? Maria needs her friends, and I am one of them, you aggravating oaf." She huffed again as she marched inside, her reticule swinging from her fingers as if she wished to swing it at him.

"Do excuse me while I check on my wife." Ashten strolled past him, his step far too lively. "When you're both ready to join us, Ellie and I will be enjoying afternoon tea in the drawing room. Like civilized people do." His friend deserted him, disappearing right out the door.

"You shouldn't be here, Sophia." He glared at her, hoping to get his point across, that he didn't appreciate her visit, not in the least. "I have vengeance to seek for my father and brother's death, vengeance I won't allow you to be a part of."

"I've gathered that by your dismissive attitude, but you must consider Maria's needs as well. She grieves deeply for your lost family members, just as you do, and I must continue to be at her side as needed. What kind of friend would I be otherwise?" She came around his desk and jabbed a finger in his chest. "I wish to be your friend as well, if you'll allow it."

"Gentlemen don't keep female friends. I wished you an enjoyable Season, that you not feel beholden to me, in any way at all. I've been gone for two months. Do you not wish for marriage and children one day?"

"Yes, not that that's any of your business, not when you tossed me aside so ruthlessly." She jabbed him again. "I wish I could hate you, James, but unfortunately I can't turn my emotions off as easily as you can."

"I'd appreciate it if you did hate me."

With a fierce growl, she stomped on his foot.

"That's a good start." He tried not to flinch.

"You deserved that."

"Of course, I did." He stepped back in case she thought to stomp on his foot again, a smile tugging annoyingly at his lips. Dash it all, but her fighting spirit was a sight to behold and he enjoyed seeing it rise.

"Now we've got that detestable moment out of the way, I must enlighten you about another matter. Your father and I came to an agreement while you were away."

"Pardon?" His brows perked up. His father had certainly been saddened by his decision to end his courtship with Sophia, although he'd also understood why he'd needed to do so. "What kind of agreement?"

"Might I take a seat while I inform you?" She gestured to the blue settee framed by the darker blue silk wallpaper of his study.

"If you must."

"James Hargrove!" Her eyes went wide, her mouth gaping. "I've never known you to be so rude."

Neither had he, but his rudeness stemmed from his current frustration, particularly at having her so close and being unable to touch her. His fingers itched with the need to hold her hands in his and press a kiss to her gloved knuckles.

"You need a stern talking to." She crossed to the settee and sat with a flourish, her lacy wrap looped behind her back and the trailing ends pooling on the padded seat either side of her.

"My apologies. Begin," he said with a flick of his fingers in the hope she'd take that gesture as *please, make this conversation quick.*

"Still rude." She lifted her sweet little chin and eyed him defiantly down her nose. "Firstly, your father was worried about your sister. He asked if I might guide and mind Maria, what with it being her first Season and your mother gone these past three years. I, of course, promptly agreed to his request. I adore Maria and in truth consider her more like a sister than a friend, just as my own sisters, Ellie and Olivia are."

"I see." Well, he couldn't fault Father's choice of minder for his sister, but Sophia's aid with Maria's first Season was now no longer necessary. It would be another year before she could enter a ballroom, her need to grieve properly, imperative. "I had actually intended on sending

Maria to our country estate for a few months while I ran my investigations, but when I broached the idea to her, she told me quite adamantly that she won't leave my side. She wishes to remain here in town."

"Which is most understandable. We all need our loved ones close at a time like this. May I speak with Maria today? I haven't seen her as yet, or is she keeping to herself for a reason?" His feisty lady smiled like an angel, her golden curls bobbing in loose waves, curls he wanted to wind around his fingers so he could tug her to him.

"She is, in fact, resting." Hopefully his answer was unarguable. He certainly kept his tone as bland as possible.

"Oh, well, I had hoped to see her. I miss her dreadfully."

"Clearly, you can't. Woodman!" he bellowed as he stuck one finger under his black cravat and loosened it a touch. His butler was never far away, and he needed his man right now.

A clatter of footsteps pounded up the stairs and Woodman swept in and halted before him, his hands clasped behind his back and the silvery streak at his brow, falling forward. "My lord, you called?"

"Yes, please escort Lady Sophia downstairs so she might enjoy refreshments with the duke and duchess."

"Indeed, I shall." A clip of his polished heels as he awaited Sophia to rise. "My lady, please follow me."

"No, I'm not yet done meeting with his lordship." Sophia brushed Woodman off with a stunning smile. "Let Their Graces know I shall be downstairs soon."

"I, ah—" Woodman lobbed him a look. His butler had never defied one of his orders to date, and now with Sophia contradicting his request so beautifully, it had his man at a quandary.

He released a long and loud sigh. "Return when I next call," he instructed his man and Woodman let out a relieved breath and vanished out the door.

"Sophia, is that you? Did I hear your voice?" Maria swept into his study, her long brown locks falling in gentle waves down her back, directly underneath her veil, her mourning gown strictly black. "You are here. How wonderful you've come for a visit."

"Your obstinate brother has finally allowed my entrance." Sophia rushed across and engulfed his sister in her arms. She kissed both Maria's cheeks and squeezed her tightly to her. "Oh, how I've missed you this past week. How have you been, my dear one?"

"I've missed you terribly too." Maria hugged Sophia back, tears welling in her eyes. "My brother has become a guard dog since his return. I feared I might never see you again."

"His bark is worse than his bite, thankfully." Sophia shot him a challenging look, the little minx. "Your brother and I have now come to an understanding, of which he shall allow me to visit, as often as you'd please. Isn't that correct, Lord Donnelly?"

"No."

"Oh dear, we must rid you of that nasty bite." A tut-tut from Sophia.

"Now who is being rude?" He wasn't going to win this argument, but that didn't mean he wouldn't go down without a jolly good fight.

"You don't wish for your sister to hold onto the

treasured friendship she and I have?" His lady linked arms with his sister, both of them giving him a rather disdainful look.

By Jove, he'd gone down already.

With a nod, he grumbled, "Lady Sophia, if you wish to visit my sister, please come as often as you'd like. Just ensure you have a suitable escort when you do."

"Thank you, and I certainly shall." Smiling wide, she returned her gaze to his sister. "We shall enjoy the sunshine and delightful conversation whenever you wish. I almost brought Beast with me today."

"Winterly's new hunting dog?"

"Yes, he's growing by leaps and bounds and is so incredibly playful. He adores it when I toss a stick. He fetches it and drops it directly at my feet."

"Oh, I would dearly love to meet him. He is such a clever pup." Maria glanced at him, hope wide in her eyes. It had been far too long since his sister had been outside the house and a trip to Sophia's home would do her a world of good. It would also mean not having Sophia here for one of her visits.

"Yes, that sounds like a wonderful idea," he conceded with a nod. "You may travel as you wish, provided you take an adequate guard. Sawyer or Fuller must be with you at all times."

"I promise." A beaming smile from his sister, one he hadn't seen in far too long.

"Perfect." Sophia fixed one corner of his sister's veil then said to her, "Ellie and Ashten are downstairs in the drawing room. They'll both wish to see you, to ensure you're well."

"As I wish to see them." Maria popped a kiss on Sophia's cheek. "I do apologize for interrupting your meeting with my brother. Please continue, and I shall see you downstairs once you're done." His sister wiggled her fingers at him then dashed away. Not good. He'd been left alone with his minx again.

"All is forgiven, James." Sadness suddenly dulled Sophia's eyes, then she blinked and gave her head a little shake before swishing back to the settee. Seated once more, she brushed her skirts straight and murmured, "I've always enjoyed speaking with your father, and with you having ridden out for the front line, I garnered a great deal of comfort in being near him."

"I understand."

"Do you truly?" An exquisite arch of her brow.

"Yes, more than I could ever express with words." He crossed to his gold and blue striped wingchair, one of his father's favorite pieces, then eased down and settled both hands on the armrests. "Is there something you wished to tell me in regard to your time with my father?"

"There most certainly is." A deep breath. "The day before your father's passing, he and I sat together in the library downstairs. We chatted about a number of things, but he also spoke of the *Fortune Maria*, his vessel having sailed into port earlier than expected, that Captain Lewiston had brought in additional cargo from a sunken vessel, including a chest containing a great deal of treasure. I can't seem to shake that conversation from my mind and it unsettles me. I wished to speak to you about it."

"I'm aware of the chest and suspect it has something to do with their deaths, except I'm not sure in what way."

"Your father said the chest was found on a Spanish galleon that capsized along a reef bordering the Spanish empire in the Americas. His excitement over the find was palpable, although I didn't get the chance to ask him exactly what was included within the chest."

"I can enlighten you, if you wish." No harm could come to her if she knew what had been contained within it.

"Please do." She leaned forward, her gaze absolute on his. "What kind of treasure was uncovered?"

"Father kept a tally of each piece in his private journal. Let me fetch it." Plucking a key from his inner black silk waistcoat pocket, he rose and collected his father's journal from his locked desk drawer. He returned to Sophia, sat next to her and opened the journal to the last two pages of entry. With the journal spread half across his lap and half across hers, he allowed her to read for herself his father's handwritten script which flowed smoothly from line to line. He read silently along with her.

Twenty-five jade pieces of various carved artifacts.
(Listed individually on the following page.)
Forty-six gold coins.
Forty feet of gold chain.
Sixty feet of silver chain.

"Oh goodness, that's a veritable fortune," she whispered as she perused the log, the low neckline of her gown dipping and exposing a small heart-shaped mole which sat so tantalizingly over her left breast, right where her heartbeat pulsed.

With her sweet white rose scent swirling around him,

his trousers tightened. His cock had always hardened when he was this close to her, his deep desire for her a craving of his very soul. Hell, he should insert some space between them.

Clearing his throat, he shuffled across an inch and—

"Are you all right, James?" She laid a hand on his jacketed arm, stilling his move.

"Donnelly," he stated firmly.

Hurt flickered in her eyes. "Are you all right, Donnelly?"

"I will never be the same again. When one loses a family member, they lose a part of their very heart."

"Yes, that's true." She tucked her hand back in her lap. "Might I ask what happened to the treasure? You said you suspect it has something to do with their deaths."

"Mr. Taylor notarized the items, then my father delivered the certified list to the War Office in Whitehall, directly into Colonel Lord Heall's hands so the treasure might be returned to the Spanish authorities who should have received the chest in the first place had their vessel not sunk."

"That was very honorable of him. Many men would have kept what they'd found for themselves."

"Yes, although the chest went missing from the War Office's locked storage room. It vanished, and the colonel hasn't been able to locate the thief or any of the stolen items." He turned the page and tapped the detailed list of twenty-five jade pieces his father had recorded of each carved artifact.

One jade necklace of small birds.

One ceremonial jade mask.
One carved ceremonial jade knife.
One skull-and-bones jade pin.
...

The list went on, and he waited as Sophia read each line. Her full lips glistened a pale pink, her long lashes sweeping down to her cheeks and back up again. "Your father has recorded that all the jade artifacts are noted as being carved by a master carver, his initials etched into each piece."

"Yes." Unable to help himself, he caught one of her golden curls, twirled it around his finger then released it. The curl bounced free before settling between her breasts, a few strands curling around the stunning heart-shaped mole.

"Donnelly?"

"Yes?" He dragged his gaze back to hers.

Her gaze softened, her next words a mere whisper, "I'm immensely glad you're home again, even though you no longer desire a courtship with me."

"If Winterly knew I currently entertained you alone in my study, he'd—"

"My brother isn't here, so you needn't worry about him." She wet her lips. "Winterly's also eager to marry me off now Ellie has wed Ashten. Don't push me away anymore, not as you've been doing since your return. This past week has been awful. Every time I knocked on your front door, Woodman sent me away with an apology."

"I can't allow any further association between us, not while there is a killer on the loose." He'd never draw her into the dark depths currently surrounding him. He shuffled about again, her nearness affecting him strongly.

"Am I making you feel uneasy?" A playful question, the little tease. "James?"

"Donnelly."

"My apologies." A long sigh. "Perhaps it's time I left?"

"I'd rather we join the others."

"Then we'll do so." Reticule in hand, she rose to her feet and with a swish of her skirts, sashayed to his door.

He closed the journal and holding it over himself, stalked to his desk. He returned the log to his locked drawer, took a few deep breaths then once assured he was in full command of his senses again, followed her into the passageway.

He halted next to her where she waited along the upper landing overlooking the main foyer below, her beautiful blue eyes as vivid in color as a summer sky and as deep as the ocean itself. "I might not be wearing my regimentals with a saber and pistol in hand, but that makes me no less suitable as your—your—never mind."

"I understand you have a murderer to uncover and justice to seek, as well as a large earldom to take the reins of, but you could use a friend at your side."

"Which is why Ashten is here."

"I wasn't referring to Ashten as that friend."

"You and I will never be friends." He stated that firmly. "You're meant for another."

She studied him, her head slanted to one side and the elegant length of her neck exposed. Everything about her intrigued him, as it always had and always would. When deep in thought, she would nibble on her lower lip and plump it up in the most distracting of ways, her sweetly innocent action always bringing a smile to his lips. She did so now, her teeth nipping into the soft flesh.

"Winterly needs to take you in hand." He crossed his arms.

"I'd rather you did that instead." She smiled, so damn endearingly. "Or are you in fear of me?"

"I fear nothing."

"You're allowing your fear to rule you. Be honest and admit it."

"There's simply too much danger for us to be together."

"You say danger, but I would say intrigue." She covered his crossed arms with both her gloved hands. "One can't live their life so questioningly. My dear brother, Harry, would say the same."

"Harry thrives on danger." Her brother served with the 18th Royal Hussars and had for several years.

"Yes, Harry loves an adventure, which I do as well." She raised up on her toes and brushed a soft kiss across his chin, since that was as far as she could reach. "Where is your adventure, my lord?"

"It has been replaced by caution and concern."

"Well, should you ever wish to embark on an adventure with me, do let me know." Grinning, she moved back a step, then turned and swept down the stairwell.

"That'll never happen," he bit out, gripping the balustrade.

"Perhaps it will. Perhaps it won't." She cast him a flirtatious glance over her shoulder and hell, he desperately wished to chase after her, to catch her against him and kiss her senseless, only that would get them both absolutely nowhere, other than in a great deal of trouble.

Trouble neither of them needed.

Trouble he wanted regardless.

Gah, heaven help him.

Chapter 2

Never had Sophia ever been quite so forward with James before, but he tempted her mischievous side like no other ever could. Heat flushed her cheeks as she hurried down the stairwell and crossed the foyer.

"Sophia, is that you?" Ellie's voice floated toward her from the yellow drawing room.

"Yes, I'm coming." She entered the room with soft yellow silk wallpaper and matching drapes of the same sunny shade. She'd sat in this room often this past year, two elegant cream settees grouped together in a way that invited cozy conversation.

"Come and sit with us." Scooting across one of those settees, Ellie's clear curiosity burned in her eyes. Her sister patted the space she made between her and Maria, her blue day dress tied with fluttering white ribbons under the high waist. "I've barely been able to sit still while you've been upstairs. I need to know everything you and Donnelly spoke about."

A chuckle from Ashten where he stood at the hearth, one hand resting on the mahogany mantel. "Please, put my dear wife out of her misery."

"I'll do my best." She sat between the ladies.

"Would you like tea or coffee during this coming inquisition?" Maria squeezed her hand and rose before crossing to a rosewood side table with drop flaps.

"Tea, please. I haven't quite garnered the taste for coffee yet, even though Winterly recently received a shipment of some exquisite coffee beans from the Province of Venezuela. The aroma is certainly divine, but nothing surpasses a hot cup of tea." She rested back against an arrangement of yellow and sky-blue cushions, while before her on the central coffee table sat afternoon tea delights arranged on two plates within easy reach.

"I prefer tea over coffee, just as you do." Maria poured hot tea from a silver tray set, her mourning veil fluttering down her back and her glossy brown curls swaying underneath the shimmer of gauze. "Cream and sugar as usual?" Maria asked her over her shoulder.

"Yes, please."

Maria stirred, and handed her the teacup without a rattle on its saucer.

At the doorway, Donnelly appeared with an irritated tug of his black silk waistcoat donned over an equally dark shirt, his jacket unbuttoned overtop and his hooded gaze on her. Sophia couldn't help but wink at him, while no one was watching, of course. Outrageous behavior, but he stirred that naughty side of her.

"Tea or coffee for you?" Maria asked Donnelly.

"I'd prefer something stronger."

Maria made a move toward the drinks' cabinet, but Donnelly stayed her with one hand and instead motioned for her to return to the settee, which his sister did. Taking a deep breath, he rolled his broad shoulders as if shrugging off his tension. Into two glasses, he poured brandy from the decanter, then joined Ashten at the mantel and handed one to him.

"Well?" Ellie whispered to her with a jab in her ribs. "Maria and I want to hear everything."

"Yes, we'll perish if you don't speak this very minute." Maria leaned in from her seated position. "The men can't hear. They're already too busy discussing politics and such."

Yes, Donnelly and Ashten now conversed about the House of Lords and the current bills being heard in parliament. She sipped her tea, and whispered, "I taunted Donnelly as ruthlessly as I could."

"You did?" Maria gasped then covered her mouth. "About what, pray tell?"

"The two of us, although he firmly believes there's simply too much danger for us to be together, so I'm afraid there shall be no return of the relationship we had before he rode out with the hussars."

"Oh dear, that is a shame." Maria slumped back. "I had so hoped you'd be my sister one day."

"One never knows what the future holds. Perhaps we still shall, but that'll depend on your brother." She gently touched her palm to Maria's cheek. "We'll have to see."

"We will always be sisters of the heart." Maria covered her hand with hers, then caught Ellie's hand too. "It is at difficult times like these that one needs their friends close. It means the world to me that you're both here."

"We shall come as often as you need." Ellie rubbed

Maria's hand. "You are very dear to us."

"Very dear." Sophia hugged Maria, her heart hurting for her dear friend and all she'd lost.

"Is all well?" Donnelly asked as he eyed his sister, worry creasing his brow.

"Yes, all is well." Maria smiled at him, although her eyes had swelled with tears and even though she tried heartedly hard to blink them away, two slipped free and trailed down her cheeks. "My heart is less burdened now that I have these two ladies here today."

"I'm glad we could ease your burden." Sophia slipped her handkerchief from her reticule, and wiped Maria's tears away.

"You don't appear less burdened." Donnelly raised a warning finger at her. "Sophia, if you continue to make my sister cry, I shall toss you out."

"You'll do no such thing." Maria made a choking sound, or perhaps it was more a restrained laugh. Yes, definitely a laugh. The sparkle had returned to Maria's eyes and the watery threat of tears now gone. With a lift of her brow, Maria continued, "So, my dear brother, what have you and His Grace been discussing while we've been nattering?"

Very clever. Maria always knew the right time to sidetrack her brother's questioning by directing the conversation back at him.

"Parliament, and the current bill being heard."

"We've also been discussing Trevithick and his interesting new invention," Ashten declared as he crossed the room, his cane in hand. He eased down onto the settee across from them. "Have you heard of him?"

"I'm not sure." Maria tapped her chin. "What has he invented?"

"The locomotive *Catch Me Who Can*."

"Oh, then I have heard of him," she bubbled as she glanced at her brother as he seated himself next to Ashten. "Father took me to see Trevithick's steam circus two years past, while you and George were in the country. It was one shilling for a ride, but Trevithick's venture suffered from weak tracks and came to a premature end. Did you get the chance to ride the locomotive?" she asked Donnelly.

"I did, before its closure, and Father mentioned taking you to visit the steam circus." Elbows to his knees, Donnelly held his brandy glass between his hands. A touch of late afternoon sunshine streaming through the wide window caught the glass and sprinkled prisms of pretty brandy-colored light across the cream carpet. "What about you, Sophia? Did you ever get the chance to visit the steam circus?"

"I visited it with Harry when he was home on leave." She touched her chest, her memory from that wonderful day with her brother warming her heart. "Afterward, he handed me Trevithick's journal to read, which is kept on the most prominent shelf in Winterly's study. Both my brothers have been fascinated by Trevithick's inventions and engineering projects. I even read about the inventor's unsuccessful attempt at driving a tunnel under the River Thames. Such a shame it collapsed. We could have used such a tunnel."

"You are well apprised about the man." Donnelly tipped a make-believe hat to her.

"I'm always eager to learn. Perhaps you could explain

what Trevithick's interesting new invention is? I'd certainly like to hear about it."

"Of course." He took a swig of his brandy. "Trevithick's been working on various ideas for improvements regarding ships, including floating docks, telescopic iron masts, as well as using heat from onboard boilers for cooking. He's even been working on detailed drawings of iron ships themselves. It's all rather fascinating."

"An iron ship? How intriguing. He's a clever man indeed if he can design such a ship to float on water." She selected a delicate cake from the afternoon tea platter, one with sunshine-yellow icing. "After I first read Trevithick's journal, I couldn't help but wonder if his steam-driven engines might one day mean travel by iron rail could become our nation's preferred choice of journeying from place to place. What do you think?"

"Steam engines are the way of the future. We shall soon be traveling by iron rail, a revolutionary new way, which will save us a great deal of time." He chose the same delicacy she had and bit into it, his hazel eyes shifting in color, the green becoming more dominant over the brown, just as they always did when his interest was piqued.

She'd noted that about him the first night they'd met, during an unfortunate moment when she'd been rescuing a kitten from the branches of a tree. She'd toppled, and when he'd caught her, she hadn't missed his eyes changing color under the moonlight.

"Oh, I've just had a wonderful idea." Ellie clasped hers and Maria's hands. "The three of us should visit the British Museum. I read in the paper there's an engineering exhibit, which includes a display of Trevithick's works. We can peruse it, and all the other wonderful displays on offer."

"It's been an age since I last visited the museum and I'd adore a trip there." An excited answer from Maria. "Father always said that to expand one's mind, one must be prepared to embrace all avenues of learning. May I go, James?" she asked her brother.

"Of course. I have no issue with you visiting the museum."

"Thank you." She grinned with pleasure. "When are you both free?" she asked her and Ellie. "On the morrow, perhaps?"

"I'm certainly free then." Ellie eyed Sophia. "Does that day suit you and Olivia? She won't wish to miss out on this trip."

"That sounds perfect, and yes, we're both free. I'll inform Olivia about the museum trip when I return home."

"Then it's agreed, on the morrow it shall be." Ellie selected a pastry. "On my last trip to the museum I saw Sir Hans Sloane's enviable collection of curiosities, as well as a newly arrived display of Greek, Roman, and Egyptian artifacts. It kept me entertained for hours, Olivia too since she was with me. Where were you that day?" Her sister eyed her. "You weren't able to join us. I distinctly remember that."

She and James had taken a ride through Hyde Park. Six months ago that had been, the day when she and James had kissed for the first time. He'd pecked her cheek while her chaperone hadn't been looking, but still, even with the brief kiss, her heart had lifted. She'd known he was the one.

Unfortunately, his earlier words reverberated through her mind in stark contrast to that kiss. *There's simply too much danger for us to be together.*

Goodness, but she would accept any danger to be with him, if only she could make him understand that. With her lashes lowered, she breathed slowly in and out and tried to lift the heavy weight her thoughts had dumped down on her.

"She was with me." Soft words from Donnelly.

She lifted her lashes and met his gaze, a flicker of hope returning. "You remember that ride?"

"I'll never forget it."

"Neither will I." They'd had such a wonderful day. After they'd reached the park, they'd walked alongside the Serpentine, the glistening waters of the river weaving through the royal parkland. James had chosen a spot under the trees where no others could intrude on them, then flapped out a blanket. They'd sat and enjoyed a picnic and sweet conversation.

She faced Ellie with a smile. "The day you and Olivia visited the museum, I took a ride in Hyde Park with Donnelly."

"Oh, yes, that's right. I remember now." Her sister squeezed her hand. "Perhaps you and Olivia can collect me from Blackgale House in Winterly's coach, then we can drive by and pick up Maria?"

"That's a wonderful idea. We'll collect you on the morrow at eleven. Does that time suit?"

"Yes, I'll be ready and waiting."

"We're going to have such a lovely day." She chose a scone smeared in jam, a mound of cream topping it, then moaned as she took a hearty bite. "Oh, Ellie, you must try one of these scones. They rival our cook's, and no one makes them more divine than her."

"The scones do look heavenly." Ellie plucked a scone from the tray and bit into it. "Mmm, superb. Would you like a bite, Ashten?" Her sister waved the remaining half of hers temptingly at him, the cream wobbling precariously on the top.

"I shall leave you to devour your scone, but I will partake of one of these divine looking meringues." Ashten chose one of the meringues with the largest topping of cream and somehow managed to put the entire thing into his mouth. Ellie laughed and Ashten chuckled.

After finishing her tea, Sophia rose and set her cup down on the side table. Spotting a new painting adorning one wall, she strolled across and gently traced one finger along the edge of the polished wooden frame.

The picture itself held a castle with one turreted tower built high on a cliff overlooking the ocean, heather surrounding it with white clouds bobbing across a blue sky and seagulls soaring overhead. So wild, yet also serene.

Donnelly wandered across to her, glanced at the painting, then at her. "This is a new piece, one which arrived only last week, the same day I returned home."

"Since it holds a prime position in your drawing room, it must hold a great deal of value to you and your family." It had been placed for all to see.

"Value of the heart, yes. I first visited Castle Craignish as a child, and rode those Scottish clifftops with my father." His gaze softened as he soaked in the stunning image, the paint strokes gloriously wide, just as the rugged landscape was. "I don't visit the castle often enough, and now I've inherited it along with the rest of my father's property and possessions. I'm hoping to journey to Scotland in the summer when the roads are more passable, but only if I've completed my current investigations, otherwise the trip will need to wait until the next summer."

"The sea air will be good for you and Maria."

"It certainly will."

She understood his decision to unearth the killer, but he was also making plans to take himself even farther away from her once his investigations were done, and he seemed to have no issue doing so. He must truly wish to let her go. Her heart squeezed in on itself.

"Did I say something to upset you?" He softly brushed the backs of his knuckles across her cheek. "There are tears in your eyes."

"No, I'm simply thinking of your father and brother." Blinking hard, she forced the unshed tears away. "You loved them dearly and your mission to uncover the truth is a worthy one."

"They would expect no less of me, to find their killer and to ensure justice prevailed." He lowered his hand to his side.

"I'm glad you're not taking the runner's verdict as it stands." She wandered around the room toward another painting, and Donnelly followed.

"There is another newly arrived painting if you wish to see it, a portrait my father insisted I sit for before leaving with the hussars. I had it hung in the library where he always enjoyed sitting to read."

"May I see it?" The library was one of her favorite

places in this house.

"Of course, but—" He glanced at the others immersed in their conversation. "I shouldn't leave my guests."

"You don't need to show me the way." She motioned toward the side door. "Might I take the rear passageway to the library?"

"There have been renovations in the rear wing and workmen are still completing their final tasks. There's a bit of a mess to navigate." He called out to the others. "Please excuse me while I escort Sophia to the library. She wishes to see one of the paintings my father recently had commissioned. We won't be long."

"Take as long as you need." Maria waved him off then returned to her conversation with Ellie and Ashten, the three immersed in their discussion.

"Come, right this way." Donnelly opened the side door and gestured her through.

"Thank you." She walked along the passageway. "I recently borrowed one of your father's travel books and haven't returned it yet. I shall do so soon."

"Take as long as you wish with it. Which book?"

"The Voyages of Marco Polo."

"Ah, that's one of my favorites." A firm nod, his gaze tipped toward hers.

"It has kept me up at night with all its intrigue."

"As it did for me. It certainly inspires one's desire for travel to the east."

"Yes, I thoroughly enjoyed reading about the cultural riches Marco Polo showcased of China. I would dearly love to visit the lands he spoke of." She skirted around a wooden crate with tools upon it. Three men in paint splattered work shirts and dusty trousers worked in the room to the side, one whistling as he painted.

"Even though that would mean traveling along the dangerous Silk Road?" Donnelly caught her hand and threaded it through his bent elbow, then guided her around several more cans of paint and drop cloths covering the polished floorboards.

"Again, you say danger, whereas I would say intrigue alone awaits along that route."

"What about Marco Polo's decision to enter the court of Kublai Kahn? Have you gotten to that part of the book yet?"

"Yes, where he won the trust of the most feared and reviled leader of his day. Such an adventure he had." Pressing her hand to her heart, she solemnly declared, "One day I shall travel to faraway shores, to the east or to the west, and those travels will be an adventure. You are not the only one who wishes to get away from town this coming summer."

"Is that right?" he murmured, his tone teasing, one brow cocked high. "And how exactly do you intend on traveling to the east or to the west?" He slowed his step as he passed portraits of several of the Donnelly earls who'd come before him, his gaze momentarily taken by them. "There is a war, remember?"

"Yes, but one can't allow the war to dominate their lives."

"True, but one must also take every precaution to ensure their safety while traveling. Winterly will need to supervise any trip you wish to undertake."

"Or I could simply find myself a husband and ask him

to take me traveling. Never forget, that is an option." She passed a corner stand with an arrangement of fragrant white roses blooming within a stylish crystal vase, then turned the corner and walked into the library. Sunshine spilled through the elegant latticed windows overlooking the rear grassy lawn, while outside a short marble column held a wide basin atop it, water pooled within and two sparrows splashing about. She let her hand slip free of Donnelly's elbow, the man himself having gone quiet since her last remark. She strolled alongside the mahogany shelves, row after row of leather-bound books stacked upon it.

"There is the portrait." Donnelly motioned toward the painting hanging at the end of the shelves. "I expect your honest opinion on it."

"Oh my." She couldn't keep her smile at bay as she crossed to the magnificent piece. In the painting, he sat atop a sleek black stallion, his buff breeches molding his strong thighs and his riding boots buckled an inch below his knees. With his white shirt open at the neck, James Hargrove, the Earl of Donnelly, appeared wild and carefree, as she'd never seen him before. "It's absolutely stunning," she whispered.

"It's certainly unlike any portrait taken of a Donnelly earl to date." A murmur from directly behind her, then he wandered off and leaned one shoulder against the window frame. His dark brown hair was slightly mussed, the longer strands curling around his neck, his impeccably tied black cravat tugged loose at one side.

"The artist has captured your personality as well as your image in the most divine way." She clutched her rose-colored skirts and walked across the large width of the burgundy oval mat between them until she stood toe to toe with him. "You look dashing in your portrait. I could stare at it all day, James."

"Donnelly." His hazel eyes glittered.

"My apologies. I could stare at it all day, Donnelly." He seemed far too insistent she not call him by his given name as she had while he'd been courting her, which was interesting, and clearly his way of instilling even more distance between them. She arched a brow, her rebellious side rising, her desire to argue right back flaring strongly through her. "Jamaica, that's where I'd like to travel to. Your father spoke about your uncle who is stationed there with his regiment. John, he said his name was, that his brother is a major and a great deal younger than him, by twenty years. He also mentioned that his brother is currently looking for a wife, an English wife from the peerage. Perhaps you might be able to give me his address. I could ask Winterly to write to him and see if he has any interest in—"

"My uncle is certainly looking for an English wife, but it shan't be you." He caught her hand and lifted it to his lips. Gently, he pressed a soft kiss across her gloved knuckles, the look in his eyes painstakingly tender, which churned her insides into a terrible mess.

"I would make a good wife, and I adapt well to changes. I would adore living in Jamaica."

"I know what you're trying to do."

"What would that be?" She settled one hand over his heart, his skin pulsing with warmth through the layers of his clothing.

"You're trying to rile me, rather ruthlessly." He swept

one hand around to the small of her back and drew her up flush against him, his other hand resting possessively over her hip. "I wish"—he cleared his suddenly husky throat— "that you could be mine, Sophia. I need you to know that."

"You need to take the barricades you've been raising between us down."

"There is your safety to consider." He leaned in closer, his breath whispering across her lips. "I need to kiss you. May I?"

"No, I've decided only my future husband may. If you would like to apply for the position, then you may state so now, or forever regret doing so."

"Temptress." Growling under his breath, he pressed his forehead to her forehead, then growled again and brushed his mouth across her mouth.

She stopped breathing.

Goodness, his lips were so soft and warm against hers.

"Kiss me back," he coaxed as he swept the tip of his tongue across her lower lip and urged her lips to part.

She opened her mouth, touched her tongue to his and got swamped in a heady wave of pleasure. She gasped as he tasted her in return, as he stroked his tongue across her tongue then pushed deeper inside her mouth and sent her thoughts spiraling, his warm breath mingling so magically with hers.

"James…" She sighed, heat spearing through her core, his kiss divine. No man had ever made her emotions rise the way he did. He'd cast a spell over her from the first day they'd met, and now she was finally alive again. "Don't let me go."

"I've missed you too, my sweet Sophia." Another kiss,

deeper and toe-curling.

Never had she imagined such an intoxicating kiss as this could exist.

She swayed against him, wrapped her arms around his neck and clung to the only man she'd ever loved. Her breasts swelled, and her nipples scraped against the silk of her rose-colored bodice. She moaned, her desire for more swamping her.

"Do you feel it, Sophia?"

"Yes, and I have no words to explain how wonderful this moment feels. It's sublime." Her legs wobbled, her limbs all loose.

"You're so incredibly enticing." He stroked one finger down her neck, her skin so sensitive to his touch. "What have you done to me?"

"My heart is beating so fast."

"So is mine." He angled her head, swooped in again and took full command of the moment, his tongue dueling with hers in a battle of wills.

Sheer pleasure coursed through her, until she could barely breathe from the intense passion he'd stirred to full and vibrant life within her.

"I don't want you receiving any gentlemen callers," he muttered against her lips.

"Have you changed your mind and wish to stake a claim on me?"

"No, that I'll never do."

"Then you'll need to give me John's address."

"No, that I'll never do either."

"I am three and twenty, James. With Ellie's recent marriage to Ashten, it has made me a rather enticing catch and I'm not sure how much longer I can fend prospective husbands off." The truth. She had received several callers since he'd left, many of them asking her to take a walk or ride, to see if they might suit. "There is passion between us. You can't deny it."

He swallowed hard, his throat working. "I haven't had a woman in a very long time, Sophia, and it appears I'm rather randy at the moment." He stepped back from her, his hands lowering to his sides. "I shouldn't have allowed so much time to pass before taking a lover."

"Pardon?" His words shocked her, jumbling her thoughts, which had likely been his intent. Hmm, well, she could give back as good as he gave. Lifting her chin, she asked rather spiritedly, "So, did you take a lover while we were courting?"

"No, but taking one allows for a perfect liaison."

"In what way?"

"There are no expectations from either party."

Her cheeks burned, and she fanned her face. Oh dear, perhaps she shouldn't have questioned him as she had, although she had to keep the charade up now that she'd begun it. "I see."

"I'm not sure you do." He pushed her up against the bookshelf, slid his hands around her bottom and squeezed her backside through the thin silk of her rose-colored skirts. His breath left his mouth in a harsh rush, his next words all rough and rumbly. "You're not wearing any undergarments."

"Good grief. I, ah, no." How had he noticed that through her skirts?

"Would you care for a quick dalliance here in my

library?" Eyes blazing with determination, he smoothed his hands over her skirted backside. "I'll ensure no one interrupts us."

He had clearly suggested such a thing to scare her away, but she craved him, the past two months they'd spent apart tearing at her deep inside. "I could never walk away from you after such a dalliance."

"You could if you tried. I need to kiss you again." He lifted her higher and settled her bottom on the middle shelf, bringing her to eye level with him. Cupping her breasts through her bodice, he lifted the mounds until the upper swells showed, right along with a peek of her nipples. He dipped his head and buried his face between her breasts, then with one flick of his tongue under the silken scalloped edge, licked her nipple.

"Oh my." Holding his face in her hands, she released a ragged sigh. "James, this is a rather delicious way of kissing."

"Very delicious." He massaged her breasts, rubbing and squeezing each in turn, then he scraped his thumbs over the beaded tips poking through the silk.

A book crashed to the ground.

Breathing harshly, he seemed to come to his senses and slid her from the shelf. Gently, he settled her slippered feet on the floor. "I can't even scare you away with my actions."

"You have failed, terribly, I'm afraid." She'd always been stubborn, and would remain stubbornly in love with him. It couldn't be helped when her heart had already chosen him.

Carefully, she picked up the fallen book and slotted it

back on the shelf, right in amongst texts in English, Latin, and Greek, which sat side by side with journals on the sciences, agriculture, and even husbandry. She righted each and every tome she'd pushed out of alignment with her bottom.

Donnelly gnashed his teeth as he too fixed a few tomes.

She shuffled alongside the shelf and frowned at a row of Minerva Press novels all askew. She'd never pushed them out of alignment, or read them, not when they were of fiction and horror, such a heinous subject matter. One of the books was slotted in the wrong way, so she tipped it out of its place, turned it the right way and frowned at a loose piece of parchment sticking out from between the pages. She slipped it free and perused it. A drawing, quite a remarkably well sketched one too. It was of a mask, with wide eyes and an open mouth, the picture colored with a wax-based crayon of pale green, the color very close to jade. Yes, definitely jade. "James, look at this."

"What have you found?" He crossed to her and she passed him the drawing. He eyed the sketch, a frown creasing his brow. "This picture was drawn by my father."

"How can you tell?"

"He always enjoyed drawing and"—he tapped a mark on the bottom, of three periods marked in ink—"this is his signature mark, an ellipsis from the ancient Greek language. This series of three periods indicates an unfinished thought or a slight pause. Father always completed each of his drawings in such a way, his belief that no sketch was ever complete. He must have sketched this jade piece from the treasure chest."

"I wonder why he tucked this particular drawing away in this book?" She opened the book and tapped the title stamped across the first page. *"Peculiar Warnings* by Elizara Whitehall, 1796."

"I've no idea why he slotted the drawing in here, but this piece of artwork is the only visual evidence we have of one of the stolen pieces of jade." He searched her gaze. "I need to get this drawing into the right hands."

"Whose hands?" She popped the book by Whitehall back onto the shelf.

"A man by the name of Captain Bourbon."

"I've never heard of him."

"He owns a gaming hell near the docks, one called The Cobra."

"Gaming hells are hardly respectable places. Is the captain trustworthy?"

"Ashten gave me his name, so yes, he's trustworthy."

"Wait." She grasped his arm. "There has to be a good reason why your father placed this sketch within the pages of a book in your library. Do you have any thoughts as to why? It's a most unusual place to put it. He should have left it in his study where it would be safe."

"Perhaps there wasn't time for him to put it there, or some other reason. I've honestly no idea, but I intend to uncover the answer." With a fierce look in his eyes, he gave her a firm nod. "I won't rest until I have."

"Promise me you'll be careful."

"Never fear for me, Sophia."

"That is an impossible request." She'd feared for him from the moment he'd ridden out with the hussars, and she'd fear for him for all time to come. One did when love was at play.

Chapter 3

The next morning, Donnelly sat in his study chair before his oak desk. Last night, he'd written a missive to Captain Bourbon about the drawing Sophia had discovered and had Sawyer hand the letter directly into the man's hands at the gaming hell he owned near the docks. He'd requested a meeting with Bourbon, as soon as the captain was available. Certainly, the drawing seemed to have been shoved haphazardly into the book, which he should have noticed in the week since his return. Thank goodness Sophia had.

"Are you certain you don't wish for a glass, my lord?" Woodman waited at attention inside his doorway, his concerned expression likely as grave as his own currently was.

"I'm certain. A glass will only hinder my consumption of this fine claret." He swigged a mouthful straight from the lip of the bottle he'd seized from the cellar after seeing Ashten, Ellie, and his ravishing Lady Sophia Trentbury away. Was he drowning his sorrows over letting Sophia go? Yes. Was it helping? No.

Allowing himself to be alone with Sophia had been a terrible mistake. He hadn't been able to keep his hands off her, or it seemed his mouth. He frowned as their time together yesterday afternoon rushed through his mind. From the moment he'd touched his lips to hers, he'd gotten lost, while her admittance that she wished to travel to Jamaica and wed his uncle had completely disarmed him. He wanted to travel the world with her, to visit faraway places that only two lovers could.

Yes, he wanted to be her husband, his soul-deep need for her as strong as ever. Unfortunately, he couldn't, not with his currently difficult circumstances. Maintaining her safety was imperative.

Another swig and he tossed the empty flagon in his wastebasket.

It hit with a clink as it knocked the other two empties. "Woodman, have a bath readied for me, then breakfast served in the dining room after I've bathed. Also, ensure Parker is aware I need the carriage brought around at the strike of nine. I'm due to collect the Duke of Ashten at Blackgale House at half past the hour, so we can spend the day going through my father's files at the docks."

"I'll organize everything now, my lord." With a tug of the cuffs of his impeccable gray jacket, his butler disappeared out the door to see to his instructions.

The man was irreplaceable, always on hand and never questioning a request.

Quite the opposite to Ashten's butler. His friend often grumped and grizzled about his man, Gorman, that his butler never knew when to keep his nose out of his business. Ashten though had come into his title at a very early age, a mere five when his parents had passed away in a tragic accident, Gorman attending him ever since.

As his father's second born son, James had never expected to receive the title or the lands he had. It had always belonged squarely to his brother and—damn it, but he missed George and always would.

His brother might have been five years older than him, but they'd always been close, finding mischief together no matter their age.

At twelve, it had been George who'd partnered him in their lessons with the saber, even though his brother was so much stronger. George had held back on his strength to ensure their sparring sessions remained a learning experience rather than a sound beating.

George had also been there the first night he'd over imbibed on whisky at a tavern, and fallen off his horse on his ride home. Sixteen, he'd been at the time, his brother dragging him over his saddle in front of him and sneaking him in through the servants' entrance, so their father would never discover his completely and utterly foxed state.

At eighteen, it had been George who'd taught him how to enchant the ladies. His brother had been rather popular within Society and intended on taking a wife before the end of this year. George would have made a wonderful earl.

Instead, he now had to fill some rather large shoes, and without a wife at his side to aid him. What he wouldn't give for his wife to be Sophia.

With his sweet minx reigning supreme in his mind, he drew forth a leaf of parchment and set about writing her a letter, as he'd done every day since they'd met, not that he'd ever dispatched any of those letters to her, or told her about them. No. Writing down his deepest thoughts had been a way for him to remain close to her, healing words which he allowed to flow from his mind onto paper right now.

My dearest Sophia,

Yesterday I succumbed to your charms and took liberties with you that I shouldn't have. I would beg your forgiveness for doing so, a hundred times over if I could, but unfortunately being the cad I am, I would gladly take advantage of you all over again if you so placed your ever-desirable self within my striking distance. Since the moment we met at the Bradford's ball, I've been smitten with you. You hold a warmth in your heart that I adore, will always adore.

Do you remember our first meeting?

I'll never forget it.

While the music had played in the ballroom and everyone danced, I stepped outside for some fresh air and there you were in the garden, a golden-haired enchantress standing atop an overturned wooden pail at the base of an oak tree, moonlight shimmering down over you. You wobbled precariously as you tried to rescue a kitten which had gotten stuck between two branches.

Such a bewitching sight you made.

Then of course you lost your balance and I had to bound over bushes to get to you, which thankfully I did. You toppled with the scrawny wee kitten in hand, and I snatched you up in my arms. Your sweet white rose scent surrounded me, just as it did yesterday while we were together in the library.

That night so long ago, I rescued a treasure. My treasure.

Unfortunately, now isn't the right time for us.

It might never be, and I've accepted that.

It would help it you did too.

Certainly, your offer yesterday to aid my sister during her time of mourning touched my heart, although your offer also sent a spear of wild and savage jealousy tearing through me. I too wish to spend such blessed time alone with you, as my sister soon shall.

Please know that you are, and always will be, the holder of my heart.

Yours forever,

James.

With his missive penned, he dribbled hot red wax and pressed his Donnelly ring into the seal then added the letter to the wooden box in which he stored all his letters addressed to her. Letters which she'd never see.

She was the only woman he'd ever wanted, quite fiercely at times, but the futility of wanting her during this difficult time wasn't acceptable. It might take years for him to uncover all he needed to in his current investigation. He certainly hoped it didn't, but his duty right now was inescapable. He had to unearth his father and brother's murderer, ensure justice was served, as well as take care of his sister during these difficult days as they mourned.

With a deep breath, he pushed back his chair and strode upstairs to ready himself for the day ahead. Each day these past two months, he'd done so with a deep longing in his heart to have all his family surrounding him, his mother who he and Maria had lost three years ago, and now his father and brother.

All three of them gone forever, but never forgotten.

Always, he'd hold them in his heart.

He closed his bedchamber door, while Woodman stood at his dresser and removed his clothing for the day and laid it on the bed, the ornate blue and gold brocade canopy tied back with matching tassels at the bedposts.

Boots shucked, he lobbed the rest of his clothes into Woodman's arms as his man stepped up to him, then he crossed to his tub and sank into the blessed warmth of the steaming water. The fire crackled and warmth flowed through his chamber.

He scrubbed himself with a bar of sandalwood soap, dunked his head and when he came up, cleaned his hair. Done with his bath as quickly as he could, he rose to his feet in the tub and waited as Woodman poured a pail of warm water over his head. Suds sluiced down his body and pooled around his ankles.

From the chair next to the hearth, he snagged the drying cloth and wrapped it around himself then stepped clear of his bath. A quick dry and he donned a pair of his favorite buff breeches, buttoned his shirt and faced his man, who knotted his cravat with practiced ease and speed to the task. Black jacket shrugged on and his boots laced, he collected his pistol from his drawer and slid it into his pocket.

Downstairs, he trod, counseling himself once more as he'd done each day since he'd become the Earl of Donnelly. The killer would pay for his crimes, and it was his duty above all else to see that done.

In the dining room, he sat and laid a napkin over his lap.

He partook of a hearty breakfast of eggs and bacon, followed by fresh bread rolls and a steaming pot of hot chocolate, a splash of brandy lacing his cup which Woodman poured into it. As he ate, he read the newspaper, his man leaving after he'd raised a thankful hand and dismissed him.

"Good morning, my dear brother." Maria swished into the room.

Shocked, all he could do was stare at her.

For the past two months, she'd only ever broken her fast in her chamber by taking a tray.

Since his return a week past, she hadn't joined him even once, no matter his request she did. She'd sent her apologies, which he'd accepted.

Yesterday's visit from Sophia had truly worked wonders.

There could be no other reason for her return to the dining room table.

He hoisted to his feet, pulled out the padded burgundy chair closest to his chair and motioned for her to sit. This morning she'd dressed not in full black as she usually did, but in a muted shade of dove-gray with white trim around the cuffs of her blouse and hem of her skirts. A yellow rose was pinned to her blouse, right over her heart, a nod to his mother's love of the same flower, while her dove-gray veil flowed overtop of her brown locks twisted into an elegant chignon.

Heart brimming with gratefulness, he kissed the top of her head as she took her seat. "You look lovely today.

Father and George would approve of your choice of clothing. They'd never wish for either of us to grieve so deeply each and every day, but instead to remember how they lived their lives to the fullest, and for us to do the same."

"Yes, and this morning I awoke with the fierce need to sit with you so I might break my fast, provided you have no issue with my returned company?" Rosy cheeked, she smiled teasingly, which brought forth his own smile.

"As long as you don't hog all the hot chocolate, then I should be able to manage."

"You are the one who always hogs the hot chocolate." She poured herself a generous cupful of the steaming brew and stirred in a teaspoon of sugar. After a sip and a heartfelt, "Mmm, delicious," she asked, "Are you still meeting Ashten this morning and driving to the docks?"

"Yes, I would appreciate his keen eye as I go over Father's papers at the warehouse offices. The Fortune Maria is also due back in port today or on the morrow, and I wish to be there when Captain Lewiston sails in." Lewiston had left London before his father and brother had passed away and he wouldn't be aware of what had happened while he'd been at sea. The captain would be shocked, no doubt, just as they'd all been on hearing the news.

"You'll be careful, won't you? With your investigations at the docks, that is?"

"Of course, and the duke is a crack-shot with his pistol should we encounter any rough sorts. I'd like to think I'm not a bad shot either. I can certainly defend myself should that be necessary." He patted the pocket of his breeches, the familiar feel of his pistol reassuring.

"Have you received word from Uncle John yet?" She buttered a roll and bit into it.

"No, and it could be weeks before he learns of Father and George's death, then several more before we receive correspondence from him."

"I've always longed to travel to Jamaica and visit him. Our uncle's letters describe the island as a veritable whirlpool of cultures colliding." A radiant smile lifted her lips, excitement ringing in her tone. "It has been so long since he was last here."

"I'm not sure how he survives the heat. Jamaica is intolerably hot compared to England."

"You're so fortunate to have spent three months with him before traveling deeper into the interior of the Americas. I wish I could have gone with you." She leaned forward, her brown eyes glittering. "Tell me all about that trip two years ago."

"Well, Jamaica is stunning, and the beaches are white with palm trees dotted all along the coastline." His father had asked him to visit each of the ports along their coastal route of the Americas where they traded, which he had. "The land is exotic, with sugarcane growing profusely. You will get to travel there one day, I'm sure."

"What of the pirates?" Excitement bubbled from her. "Are they as rowdy and unruly as I've heard? Did you ever encounter any?"

"Yes, the islands of the Caribbean are home to a great nest of pirates. They swagger about the streets, trafficking their outlandish loot to merchants and other buyers. They fill their pockets with gold, then squander their bootie in the gambling rooms, then they carouse and brawl. They're filled with bloodlust, always searching the seas for one hefty prize or another." He tapped her nose then resumed reading his newspaper. "Should a pirate ever come across you, you'd be a prize he'd seek to capture and never return."

"Father used to warn me that if I misbehaved, he'd send me to Uncle John. I think that made me want to misbehave even more, so I could see the island our uncle calls home." Grinning, she snuck the butter knife from the slab of butter and swung the short-curved blade back and forth like a sword. She slashed one corner of his paper then stabbed right through the middle. A giggle as she pressed her nose to the paper and batted one eye through the slot. "Give me yer treasure, me hearty, or ye'll walk the plank."

His sister's playfulness had returned, and he couldn't be more grateful.

Chuckling, he folded the paper and tapped it on her head. "If ye keep misbehaving then ahoy, to the high seas ye'll go."

"You can heave ho." She stabbed her knife into a fresh roll and tore a bite off the bread.

"You have lost all decorum."

"I wouldn't mind meeting an actual pirate." Another tearing bite.

"You would change your mind rather fast if you did."

"There must be a good reason why pirates have chosen a wicked path over an honorable one. Maybe they had no choice but to plunder in order to survive. Everyone deserves the chance for redemption, even pirates. Don't you agree?"

"No." He plucked her stabbed roll, spread butter and preserves on it and chewed. "Are you looking forward to your trip to the museum?"

"Exceedingly." She raised a brow, chin propped in her upturned palms. "You could join us later in the day if you finish your investigations before it gets too late. I'd adore it, as I'm sure Sophia would too."

"Joining you, Sophia, and her sisters won't be possible." He couldn't place himself within sniffing distance of the lady who tempted his desires as no other ever could, otherwise he'd be sneaking her into a side room and stealing kisses from her as he had yesterday. A repeat of that incident would be dangerous. Exceedingly dangerous.

"I'm certain you'd have fun."

"Having fun is the problem."

"Ah, excuse me, my lord." Woodman stood in the doorway, a smile rising as he spied Maria at the table. "I do beg your pardon for the interruption. Your carriage is ready at nine as requested."

"Excellent. Fetch my greatcoat and hat, Woodman." He rose and pressed a kiss to Maria's cheek. "I've thoroughly enjoyed breaking my fast with you. I'll be home at eight for dinner, and we can discuss pirates and the saving of their horrid souls further then."

"Be sure to observe all you can at the warehouse and report back to me on all you uncover." Brow arched, she handed him a shiny red apple from the center of the table, a favorite fruit of his.

"Are you an investigator now?" He pocketed the apple for later.

"No, but I need to be aware of what's going on. I've been wallowing in my grief and not being as present as I should be. You and I only have each other, and I intend to be the best sister ever."

"You're my only sister, so being the best is already guaranteed, although I'll inform you about all that I uncover at dinner tonight, provided you inform me about all you observe today at the museum. If you don't regale me with fascinating tales, then I shan't share a thing with you." With long strides, he crossed to the door and with one last glance over his shoulder, winked at his sister. "And by fascinating tales, I mean regarding Sophia. I need to keep an eye on her at present, and no, you may not ask why."

"Why?" She laughed.

"You're an impossible imp."

Her continued laughter followed him out the front door, his sister's good humor once more returned to him. His heart swelled with happiness.

Chapter 4

Sophia paced her bedchamber from wall to wall, her white linen nightgown brushing her bare toes. After leaving James yesterday, worry had battered at her every second since. Whether he liked it or not, she would aid him in whatever way she could, and that included being there for both him and Maria. He couldn't kiss her then send her on her way. No, she simply couldn't turn her emotions off at the drop of a hat, not when her very heart and soul desperately hungered for more time with him.

Mama had once said that some men needed a gentle push, and it appeared James more so than any other. Before he'd left for the war, he'd always been there for her, charming her with his quick wit, showing her his love by his devoted attention, and yesterday in his library, he'd gifted her with his passion, his kisses fierce and soul-entwining. She'd always known when they came together in such a way it would be explosive, and it certainly had been.

A knock rattled her door and her maid peeked around it with a tray in hand. "Good morning, my lady. I heard your footsteps. Do you wish to break your fast?"

"Yes, I'm famished. Do come in."

"The bread is fresh from the ovens, the butter churned earlier this morn." In her white aproned skirts, her maid placed the tray on the corner table under the window and swished her red-gold drapes open, the color matching that of her bedcovers.

She eased into the chair at her table and sipped her tea, the brew perfectly milky and sweet. Her bread roll had already been sliced in two, so she buttered it and spread raspberry jam atop. Eyes closed, she bit into its light and airy warmth and moaned her approval. Sweetly delicious.

"Would you like me to lay out your clothes for the day?"

"Yes, I'm to visit the British Museum and wish to wear my favorite pale blue woolen skirt and matching jacket. Set them on the bed, Abby."

"What a wonderful choice." Her maid poked about in her closet then swung back to her four-poster bed and set her jacket and skirt on her plush bedcovers, the soft golden drapery of her canopy fluttering down each side.

While she ate, her maid whooshed about, tidying her chamber.

Birds chirped from the large elm trees overlooking the driveway and she leaned one elbow on the windowsill as she polished off the rest of her roll. Mornings had always been her favorite time of the day, particularly the dawn hour when the birds awoke, and the skies lightened. She always fantasized about the day ahead. Today appeared more gray and dismal than yesterday though, when she'd enjoyed a walk about James's gardens. Gray clouds still hid the sun from view, although a speck of blue poked teasingly through here and there. Likely it would rain, as it so often did in London, no matter that spring had sprung. She rested back in her chair and asked her maid, "Is anyone else up and about?"

"Yes, Lady Olivia is breaking her fast in the dining room with his lordship."

On her return from Donnelly House, she'd spoken to her younger sister and Olivia had been excited about their proposed trip to the museum today. She and her sisters would ensure Maria knew that they'd always be there for her. She'd also spoken to Winterly, Mama, and Olivia about James's decision to hire Captain Bourbon to aid him in his investigations. Winterly had thought it a sound idea, having already heard about Bourbon and his specialist abilities from Ashten some time ago. Since Ashten trusted the man, so did her brother.

Finished with her breakfast, she stood and her ever-efficient maid swished in behind her, drew her nightgown over her head and within mere minutes had her clothed in her pale blue woolen skirt and matching jacket, a cream blouse buttoned underneath and her leather-soled slippers on. She sat in her chair before her mirrored dressing table, while Abby arranged her hair in a top knot with a few loose curls dangling down each side.

Another knock on the door and Olivia breezed in wearing a lavender walking dress with long sleeves and white lace adorning the scalloped neckline, a parasol in one hand and her reticule in the other.

"Good morning, you look delightful in that color." Her sister brushed a kiss across her cheek, first one and then the other. "Pale blue suits you to perfection."

"It's James's favorite color on me." Which she didn't mean to blurt out, but her thoughts were consumed by him.

"It's interesting you should say that." A knowing grin tugged at the corners of Olivia's lips as she perched on the end of her bed and delicately crossed her legs. "I wonder how *your* James is doing this morning? I'm so glad you told us all about his investigations last night. Hiring Captain Bourbon, the spymaster, all sounds rather thrilling. Hopefully Donnelly will find exactly what he's looking for, and sooner rather than later."

"I hope so too, and *my* James better be taking all care and not coming to any harm during those investigations." Yesterday, before she'd left Donnelly House, he and Ashten had confirmed that they'd travel together this morning to the docks, so James might sort through his father's papers at his warehouse, while Ashten offered his aid.

"Oh, and speaking of taking all care," Olivia gushed. "Captain Poole has arrived and is currently speaking with Winterly in his study. I asked Captain Poole if all was well across the channel and he said the hussars are taking all care, including Harry."

"That's good to hear." Any news they received about Harry eased their minds. At present their brother was stationed near Spain's land border with France, right in the middle of the fiercest fighting. These were difficult days for certain as their regiments stood alongside the Spanish in Spain's endless battle to retain their land. Every week the published lists in the papers reported more deaths of English soldiers who would now never return to their families. The Corsican surely had to be halted, which seemed an almost impossible task at times with the sheer number of men he retained in his fighting force, but they'd never lay their weapons down, nor give Napoleon the chance to cross the channel and attempt to take their great land for himself.

"Harry would want us to think only about winning the war, and not fearing for him while he fought," Olivia said with a thoughtful nod. "You're thinking about him, just as I am. I can tell."

"He's never far from my thoughts." She didn't doubt that Harry awoke every morning in a dangerous place, that he fought with strength and bravery to remain alive, and that his only desire was to ensure England retained its freedom during these dark days of oppression.

A yap echoed and paws scratched at her door, followed by a heartfelt mewl that melted her heart.

Beast, their wee puppy—who had a basket in Harry's room across the hallway and slept there each night, so he would know their brother's scent—raced inside as Olivia opened the door. He skidded across the polished floorboards, slid under Sophia's skirts and knocked into her ankles.

She got licked, his wet nose tickling.

Giggling, she tipped her face toward Abby as her maid rouged her cheeks and dabbed beeswax on her lips, then while Abby tidied everything away inside her dresser box, she scooped a still licking Beast free from under her skirts and hugged him. "You are such an eager pup, and a complete delight. Harry will adore you, when you two finally get to meet."

"He's so mischievous too." Olivia leaned in and petted between his silky ears with a soft coo. "Oh my, you are going to make a wonderful hunting dog when we visit the country. Winterly Manor is surrounded by fields and wonderful fresh air. You'll need to take care though, not to get lost in the long grass. You must grow taller and stronger."

Abby dipped her head to Sophia. "Is there anything else you need, my lady?"

"Yes, take Beast and ensure he's fed. Fill his bowl well. We need him to grow." She snuggled her nose in his furry neck, kissed the top of his head, his sweet puppy scent enveloping her, then carefully, she handed the pup across.

Smiling, her maid disappeared out the door cuddling their pup.

"Should we see how Mama is before we leave?" Olivia adjusted her wrap. "With her bedchamber next to mine, I heard her coughing during the night. I asked the cook to prepare her a posset of hot milk spiced with wine then sat beside her as she drank it. It certainly soothed her throat and she settled back to sleep far easier."

"Let's check in on her now, before we leave." If Mama needed them to remain then they would. Family came first, as Mama had always taught them. She scooped her bonnet and gloves, linked arms with Olivia and marched out the door toward Mama's bedchamber.

A rap on the door and when Mama called out for them to come in, she walked inside with Olivia and assessed Mama as she crossed to her. Propped up with her pillows fluffed behind her, Mama's golden hair wisped with strands of silver were hidden under her lacy nightcap. Her face was pale, but not overly so, and she smiled as she held her beloved embroidery in hand.

"Well, you two look delightful today. I wish to hear all about your excursion when you return." A stitch and a look that said, *I'm on the mend. Don't fuss over me.*

"How do you feel this morning?" Fuss, she would. Sophia brushed a kiss across the top of Mama's head and perched on the bed beside her.

"The posset Olivia brought me last night soothed my throat, although I wouldn't mind remaining abed for the day and napping as needed. Please do not say you wish to watch me sleep." A teasing arch of one brow. "Actually, your papa always told me I talked quite animatedly in my sleep, that I can hold quite the conversation. Perhaps you might like to stay."

"I've actually heard you talking from time to time." Olivia tapped the wall between her bedchamber and Mama's. "The walls are far too thin in this part of the house."

"Yes, far too thin, and you've received my ability to natter while napping, Olivia dear. I've heard you from time to time too." A wag of Mama's finger.

"I do?" Olivia's eyes went wide. "I had no idea."

"I would never speak a mistruth, and it's quite a delightful ability to hold. Be proud of it." Mama looped her blue thread through the cotton, the artful stitching of a skyline clear to see above a burgundy rose garden with thick greenery. Mama had been working on the piece for a number of months, the landscape a stunning portrayal of her beloved gardens. Lifting her gaze and eyeing her,

Mama murmured, "My dear Sophia, I've been thinking about your current situation with the Earl of Donnelly, and I can see from the look on your face and the depth of need in your voice when you speak about him, that your feelings for him will always hold firm."

"I love him, Mama." She had no issue speaking the truth, or for any of her family to know that there could be no other for her, other than James.

"Your beau is so much like your dear papa in nature, never willing to leave any stone unturned when it comes to family and matters of the heart. You will never be able to give him up, and with that being the case, we must come up with a plan." A firm look. "One can't live their life in fear, which you must never forget."

"I have a plan in mind." Nibbling on her bottom lip, she smoothed her pale blue skirts. "I'm not sure you'll agree with it though."

"Do tell." Mama waved her to continue.

"Yes, do tell," Olivia demanded as she sat on Mama's other side.

"I intend to keep the Earl of Donnelly on his toes, to ensure he knows he can confide in me, and to always be there to support him, his sister as well."

"That will surely show your devotion and love, your desire to be the lady who stands at his side too. That is a sound plan." A confirming nod from Mama before she glanced at her sister and gently touched her palm to Olivia's cheek. "Even though you're my youngest, and possibly the most mischievous of my three daughters, I need you to keep an eye on Sophia for me."

"I shall, Mama." Olivia kissed Mama's cheek.

"Very good." Mama shooed them with a swish of her hands. "I wish you both a wonderful day, and give Ellie a hug from me."

"We will." Sophia closed the door behind her and Olivia, then stomped a little too loudly down the hallway. "I can't believe Mama told you to keep an eye on me."

"Someone must, and the task has fallen to me for now." Olivia skipped along merrily beside her.

"I can keep an eye on myself." Downstairs, she marched.

"Yes, but you do find trouble far too easily. Hopefully I can keep you out of it."

"Heavens, Sophia. You have extremely loud footsteps today." In gray trousers and a blue jacket fitted smoothly across his broad shoulders, Winterly emerged from his study and waited at the base of the stairs. He pulled both her and Olivia into his arms, his hug as wonderful and all-encompassing as Papa's had always been. "Are you two ready for your day at the museum?"

"Yes." She squeezed him back. "We'll collect Ellie on our way to Donnelly House."

"I'll have Jeeves bring the coach around." He gestured toward his study as he strode away, his gaze on them over his shoulder. "Keep Captain Poole company while I do. I shan't be long."

"Of course." She'd always enjoyed speaking to Captain Poole. She swished into her brother's private domain and Poole rose from one of the two forest-green padded chairs in front of Winterly's chunky oak desk.

Hat in one hand, he swept into an elegant bow before her, his regimental uniform of royal blue, silver and white impeccably pressed. "Good morning to you, Lady Sophia, Lady Olivia," he added as her sister stepped in beside her. "Who I've already had the good fortune of spending some time with this morning."

"As I have with you, Captain." Olivia motioned toward her. "I've already spoken to my sister and shared your news that Harry's doing well."

"I do have more news if you'd like to hear it," he offered.

"Yes, please, and welcome home, Captain Poole." Sophia was eager to hear any news about Harry that he could impart. "We miss our brother dearly. Can you speak of Captain Harry Trentbury's current orders?"

"Major Harry Trentbury now," he corrected with a grin. "He advanced to major three weeks past. I've just informed Winterly, which Harry asked me to do. Winterly was thrilled of course."

"Oh, how wonderful." Sophia squealed, beyond excited for her brother. "Are you home on leave for long?"

"Five days is all, I'm afraid. Major Lord Bishophale asked me to return with papers for the War Office and I ride back to Wellington on the front line at the end of the week."

Whistling cheerily, Winterly returned. "I heard the squeal which surely means you've both heard the good news about Harry?"

"Yes." Sophia clapped, as did her sister. "Mama will be thrilled when she hears of Harry's advancement through the ranks."

"Beyond thrilled, and I'll tell her shortly. Poole also informed me that Harry is about to embark on a secret

mission, his engineering skills soon to be put to the test."
Her brother rested his backside on one corner of his desk.

"That sounds intriguing. Can you tell us more?" she
asked Poole.

"Unfortunately, I can tell you only what I've told your
brother." A touch of firelight shimmered over the captain's
golden hair, his locks cropped short as many of the officers
preferred. Harry too had sported the exact same hairstyle on
his last bout of leave.

Goodness, but that had been almost a year ago now
and she dearly wished he'd be able to return home for
another visit soon. They'd all missed him dreadfully. "Is
our brother's mission dangerous?"

"Most of the missions we run are, but Harry's is
currently more suited to his inherent engineering abilities,
if you understand my meaning?" With his gaze steadfast,
he continued, "If you wish to write letters to him, I can pass
them along. I'll see Harry soon, very soon."

"Yes, we'd love to do that. Where shall we send
them?"

"Directly to me at the War Office. I'm more often
there than not."

"We'll have them delivered to you before you leave,
and speaking of the War Office, did you hear of the
treasure chest which disappeared from one of the locked
storage rooms?" She couldn't help but ask. Perhaps Poole
knew something and had additional information at hand.
"Donnelly told me it vanished, and that Colonel Lord Heall
hasn't been able to locate the thief or any of the stolen
items."

"Yes, that's true. A terrible tragedy too, Donnelly's

father and brother passing away while he was across the channel on duty. His entire regiment grieves with him."

"He wishes to uncover the killer and ensure justice is sought, his belief being that their death could be connected to the stolen chest."

"Well, if he needs my aid, I'll gladly offer it." He frowned, worry creasing his brow. "The colonel was most distressed that someone had had the audacity to sneak into the War Office and thieve that which clearly belongs to another. In this case a treasure chest belonging to the Spanish, the proceeds of which could ultimately aid them in their war. I'm surprised the magistrate hasn't investigated further, that he's concluded with the runner that their deaths were accidental."

"Their bodies were found in the river, with no outward sign of struggle." Winterly crossed his arms and tapped one foot. "That is why accidental death has been recorded. No bruising was discovered on their bodies, or wounds of any kind, and following the old earl's death, his son was in deep despair, his grief immense."

"The son's grief is expected, but not his death." Firm words from Poole. "I shall do my best to see what else I can uncover at the War Office."

"Thank you, Captain." She dipped her head.

"You're most welcome, Lady Sophia." He lifted her hand and kissed her fingers, then did so with Olivia too. "Ladies, I do hope you enjoy your day."

"Yes, I'm sure we shall." She left her brother and Poole to resume their meeting and along with Olivia donned her gloves and stepped outside where their coach awaited them.

Once seated on the plush squabs, their driver closed the door and climbed atop his perch. A slap of the reins and the carriage bumped forward, the horses soon moving fluidly as they trotted down the road.

Across town, they journeyed to the fine street Ellie lived on and pulled into the circular driveway of a mansion constructed of stone with regal columns at the front and extensive gardens to the sides and rear. Their coachman opened the door and set the step on the ground.

"Good morning." Cheeks flushed a healthy pink, Ellie accepted their driver's aid and stepped inside. She plopped down on the burgundy padded seat across from her and Olivia, laid her cloak on the squab and rearranged the folds of her red woolen skirts, the pointed toes of her half boots poking out from under the hem.

Gorman, Ashten's butler and right-hand man, settled a basket at Ellie's feet, the silvery streaks at the sides of his dark-haired head glimmering. "There are chicken sandwiches, Your Grace, an assortment of dried fruits and cheeses, lemonade, and sweet raspberry tarts. Is there anything else you might like to snack on while you travel?"

"No thank you, Gorman." Ellie sent him a glowing smile. "I'm sure you've packed enough food for an army, and I shall enjoy all the treats."

"Are you certain you don't need me to accompany you?" A little flustered, he motioned to the top of the carriage. "I could sit up top with the driver, with no issue at all."

"Oh, I'm very certain. We have yet to collect Lady Maria Hargrove who shall have a guard with her, so we will be well attended for the day." She patted Gorman's arm. "All will be well."

"Your Grace, I worry about—"

"Gorman, try to enjoy your day without worrying about me." Ellie pulled the door closed and rapped on the ceiling, dismissing Gorman as Sophia had never seen her sister do. "To Donnelly House, immediately," Ellie called.

"What was that about?" Olivia crooked her head at Ellie. "I've never seen you be so rude to your butler."

"Unfortunately," Ellie murmured as she sank back, "Ashten let it slip to Gorman that I'm enceinte."

"Pardon?" Olivia gaped. "You're with child?"

"Yes." A beaming smile from Ellie, her eyes twinkling.

"Oh my, congratulations." Sophia bounced across and smothered Ellie in her arms, then Olivia giggled as she too enveloped them, the three of them squeezed in tight on one bench seat.

Ellie laughed as she squeezed them back. "You two are the first I've told, other than for Ashten, who is a big blabbermouth. He tries to hide his grin whenever Gorman hovers over me, but I see it. My husband is ecstatic that Gorman no longer pesters him every hour of the day, but me instead. Truly and honestly, I can no longer walk two steps without tripping over Gorman. He has tracking me down to a fine art too. In fact, I suspect he's already saddling a horse and in pursuit. We shall see him at the museum and he will continue to hover over me all day, mark my words."

"A little hovering never hurt anyone." Olivia did a little jig on her bottom. "Mama and Winterly will be thrilled. Oh, and will you tell Maria today? I doubt we'll be able to keep the news in now that you've told us. You have to write to Harry too, and let him know. We're going to pen letters to him and hand them to Captain Poole before he leaves town. He's brought some papers to the War Office and intends to return to Wellington at the end of the week."

"Of course, I'll tell Maria, and how is our dear Captain Poole?"

"Very well, and likely still with Winterly in his study. Harry's now a major too." Sophia did her own little jiggle. "Poole said he advanced three weeks past."

"Oh my, how superb." Ellie grasped their hands in hers, her golden curls fluttering down her back.

The carriage rolled down the driveway and along the streets toward Donnelly House. They continued chatting, asking Ellie all about her pregnancy, how she felt and what the doctor had said. This would be the first grandchild for Mama, the first niece or nephew for her, Olivia, and her brothers. So wonderful.

As they finally turned into Donnelly's driveway, they trotted between two towering oak trees and rounded a green and white garden surrounding a graceful statue of a lady-angel dressed in a loosely draped gown, her head bent and feathery wings sweeping from her back and curving around her body, her wingtips resting at her feet. On an earlier visit, Maria had told her that her father had commissioned the piece following her mother's death three years past. Fifteen years of age Maria had been at the time, and she'd believed wholeheartedly that her mother was now an angel in heaven, which her father had decreed to be the truth, thus the statue depicting her mother as an angel with wings, always and forever with them. Such a beautiful memorial to the late Lady Donnelly.

From the front door of Donnelly House, Maria hurried out with her guard, Sawyer, who took a position on the rear platform rather than joining their driver atop the coach, and—Sophia giggled as she saw why. Gorman leaned over from up top, one finger held in a shushing motion over his lips as he eyed her through the door. Such a wily, quick man. He must have bounded up when Ellie had shut the door at Blackgale House. No need for him to saddle a horse. He was already with them.

With her head covered in a dove-gray veil that fluttered down her back, Maria enveloped them in hugs before taking the seat next to Sophia, her black fur-lined cloak swaying from her shoulders. "How is everyone this morning?"

"Very excited." Sophia caught Maria's hands in hers as the coach moved forward down Donnelly's driveway. "You'll never guess." She glanced at Ellie for permission to spill the news and when her sister nodded, she blurted, "Ellie is expecting."

"You are?" A wide grin as Maria rose from her seat and squeezed Ellie. "Congratulations."

Yes, huge congratulations were in order.

What a wonderful day.

Chapter 5

James alighted from his Donnelly coach at the docks, the gray skies overhead darkening as a storm brewed and the clatter of carts and men bustling about filled the air. He and Ashten had spoken at length on their journey to the docks and he'd fully updated his friend on the message he'd sent to Captain Bourbon, that he hoped to receive a reply soon so he might show Bourbon the drawing and hear of any information he'd uncovered. "How did you first meet Bourbon?" he asked Ashten as they weaved around others along the busy wooden walkway. "I'm immensely curious."

Ashten tapped his cane as he strode, his tan tailcoats flapping and his hat firm atop his head. "We met four years past while I was in service with the hussars. The Duke of Wellington had called a meeting, which I attended, directly before what could have been a very disastrous battle against Napoleon. Bourbon had come to Wellington with crucial information a mere twenty-four hours before we intended to attack the French. We weren't certain if we could trust Bourbon's word, but in the end, we chose to accept his information and we were most grateful we did. The battle would have been a deadly one for us, with the loss of thousands of lives, had we acted as we'd intended."

"Interesting." His regard about Bourbon lifted to a higher degree. "So, Captain Anteros Bourbon is a spymaster who fights to ensure our Englishmen don't lose their lives in this atrocious war and appears fluent in several languages, his accent not one I could correctly pick when I visited him at his establishment. Which begs the question—where exactly does he hail from?"

"If you wish to truly understand Bourbon, then all you need to know is that he will side with any nation which revolts against the French. While I served with the hussars, I saw Bourbon in talks with the Portuguese, the Spanish, and the Sicilians, speaking each of their languages in turn. His desire is to see Napoleon brought to his knees, his belief that the Corsican should never be permitted to rule all of Europe. With that being the case, he will continue to lurk within the darker depths of London's underworld to source whatever information he must to ensure Napoleon's downfall. That is where he hails from, the shadows, where he's most at home."

"I see." Well, he wholeheartedly agreed that Napoleon must be brought down. Flicking the collar of his greatcoat up against the cold wind, he passed by the murky brown waters of the Thames, this stretch of the river filled with ships and barges, their captains steering their vessels with care along the quayside. Dockworkers with caps on their heads, heaved cargo onto their shoulders and stacked it onto wheeled trolleys. Ships were being unloaded upon their arrival, while others were being loaded for their departure. His father had thrived within the hustle and bustle of this area of London, as equally as he'd thrived in attending parliament, seeing to their many enterprises and maintaining their Donnelly earldom, townhouse and country estate. The three warehouses up ahead which belonged to his father now belonged to him, and he was expected to continue what his father had begun, what he'd always expected would be George's. Still, it was his now and he would make his father and brother proud as he took the reins. He could do no less than that, in order to honor their memories.

"G'day, sirs." A lad dashed past them then skipped backward with a tip of his cap, his mop of brown hair hiding his eyes and soot smeared across one cheek. Wearing breeches with loose suspenders and a brown woolen jacket which was far too big for his scrawny frame, the lad grinned. "The cap'n says he's got more information 'bout yer drawin', and looks forward to seeing it."

"You're with Captain Bourbon? Where is he?" Donnelly checked over his shoulder, but caught no sight of Bourbon among those on the walkway. He eyed the boy again. "What's your name, lad?"

"Wills, sir." The child bounced around him, his gaze on the apple bulging from within his coat pocket, the skin a shiny red and the stalk holding a small leaf at the tip.

"Here." He rubbed the fruit on his coat, shone it some more and tossed it to the lad. "This would have been picked from one of my apple trees this morning. Enjoy."

"Thank ye." A big bite, juice dribbling down his chin. The lad turned on his heel and sprinted toward one of his brown-brick warehouses, then disappeared through the side entrance of the building housing the upstairs offices.

"Good morning, gentlemen." Bourbon strode in beside them, his beaver hat shading the top half of his dark head, his black riding breeches donned and knee-length boots polished to a high sheen. The collar of his jacket sat high and hid the lower half of his face, the elusive spymaster hiding himself even in the bright light of day.

"Bourbon, good of you to join us." He shook the captain's hand and gestured to Ashten. "I've not long heard how you two met. The duke speaks highly of you."

"As I speak highly of him when I'm given the chance." Bourbon shook Ashten's hand. "Good to see you, my friend. Word is you've recently wed Lady Ellie, sister to the Earl of Winterly. *Congratulazioni.*"

"Thank you." Ashten shook Bourbon's hand in return. "It's good to see you're well and that you've now joined us. Does this mean you've uncovered something of interest in your investigations?"

"I most certainly have." The spymaster motioned to the side door of the warehouse. "Gentlemen, let's speak inside where we can't be overheard. I have much to enlighten you both about."

"Hopefully you bring good news." Donnelly strode through the door, eager to progress on his investigations. At times, he'd feared he might never move forward, each day that had passed allowing evidence to become buried deeper. That he couldn't allow.

"Lord Donnelly!" Mr. Taylor hailed him as he strode away from several of his workers stacking crates. With a nudge of his spectacles, his man of affairs handed him the company's burgundy leather-bound ledger. "We've received cargo this morning of indigo dyes, cotton, and silk. The quality of the silk is above reproach and will fetch a handsome price at market. All is listed here for your perusal."

"Excellent, I'll read through your entries and leave the journal on my desk for you to update with the prices when received." Overseeing every element of his father's business was important, as was maintaining strict control as he took the reins. Mr. Taylor hadn't quite appreciated being inundated with so many questions this past week, not since it had caused him to get behind in his work, but he'd managed admirably all the same. Certainly, employing a clerk would help lessen Taylor's workload, but when he'd broached the subject with the man, he'd insisted he had no need of a clerk. He preferred handling everything himself, so for now, things would remain the same. "Resume what you were doing," he instructed Taylor.

"Right away, my lord." Tugging on his neckcloth, he hurried back to the workers and gestured to where he wanted the crates.

Upstairs, Donnelly followed Bourbon and Ashten who'd already walked on ahead. He marched inside the main upper floor office and halted in the center, a spillage of light trickling through the navy drapes covering the wide window, the docks and river below. Wills sat perched on the edge of his desk, one foot swinging as he munched on his apple.

Bourbon swiped the lad's cap and ruffled his hair. "Keep an eye out on the stairwell, Wills. Whistle if we are about to be disturbed."

"Aye, Cap'n." With a crunch, the lad sauntered out

and closed the door with a soft click.

Bourbon stepped past the desk, opened the drapes wider with one finger and surveyed the area outside. Seemingly satisfied with what he saw, he then allowed the drapes to fall back into place and faced them. "Donnelly, I can report that your father and brother were honorable men, both clearly intent on returning the sunken chest of treasure to its rightful owner. They believed by delivering it to the War Office, it would be returned to the authorities in Spain, although the treasure never in fact belonged to the Spanish at all. I've discovered it belonged to the Portuguese House of Braganza."

"Are you certain?" It had been recovered from a Spanish galleon.

"Yes. Two and a half years past, when the entire Braganza Dynasty of Portugal fled into exile, the treasure within the chest was left behind with the Spanish royal family, of which the Spanish promised to send the chest along when all became safe." Bourbon slipped his hand inside his jacket and removed a piece of exquisite jade. Gently, reverently, he handed the piece to Donnelly. "This is a ceremonial mask, one which I recovered in the early hours of this morning from Mr. Blackburne, a wealthy solicitor. I found the mask within his town office, with evidence that he bought the piece for a large sum from a contact of his at the eastern docks. I've yet to uncover who that contact is, but I shall. It's only a matter of time until I discover exactly who stole the chest and is now selling each item within it. Once I have that name, I'll have found your killer."

"You believe the thief and the killer are one and the

same?" He certainly did, particularly since his father and brother had no known enemies.

"I do, particularly when no one else wished them harm." Bourbon held out his hand. "Did you bring the drawing?"

"Yes, of course."

"Let's see if the mask is a match to it."

Donnelly slid the drawing from his pocket and handed it to Bourbon, who unfolded and held the parchment for all three of them to see. Definitely a match. Anticipation of what this meant thrummed through him. "We're far closer than ever before," he whispered.

"We are." Ashten closed his hand firmly over his shoulder. "You'll get the justice you seek." His friend turned to Bourbon. "The Royal Houses of Portugal and Spain are linked through marriage, are they not?"

"Yes, many times over. I can confirm the Spanish galleon that held this treasure sank on its journey to the Portuguese Viceroyalty of Brazil, where the Braganza royal family now reside. That's how I've confirmed the treasure chest's true ownership." Bourbon folded the drawing, his gaze returning to Donnelly. "I'd like to hold onto this picture for a few days. Is that permissible?"

"Of course. Return it when you no longer have need of it."

"You have my thanks." A nod as Bourbon slipped the drawing into his pocket then accepted the jade mask from Donnelly and squeezed his arm. "You mentioned in the missive you sent to me that Lady Sophia Trentbury was with you when you uncovered the drawing."

"Yes, although she is the one who actually uncovered

it, not I."

"Interesting." Bourbon arched an inquisitive brow. "This may sound like an unusual question, but do you believe in foreseers, Donnelly?"

"I haven't had the fortune to meet one. Do you believe in them?" he asked right back.

"There is a seer in Algiers who I consider family, Shira Ria. When I visited her a year past, she read my future, and spoke of two ladies I'd yet to meet, as well as a drawing and certain events that would unfold. I'm certain that this is the drawing she spoke of, and the events currently unfolding are those she warned me about. The name she gave me of the first lady was Sophia, the name of the second, Olivia.

"Sophia's younger sister is Olivia."

"Then you must excuse me while I follow Shira's advice. No time can be lost." Bourbon lifted his beaver hat and without another word, disappeared out the door.

"What advice could that be?" he asked Ashten, who simply shrugged, so he strode after Bourbon.

He halted outside the door, currently devoid of even one soul.

Gripping the handrail overlooking the stairwell and the lower floor of the warehouse, he searched for the elusive spymaster. Crates were stacked in rows with clear aisles between each row, Bourbon nowhere to be seen, the lad having vanished right along with him. So swift and fast.

"Donnelly?" Ashten called from the office. "Allow Bourbon to do his job. We meanwhile have a filing cabinet calling our names."

Yes, they did, and he'd already placed his trust in

Bourbon. He needed to allow the man to do his job. He returned to Ashten, who'd pulled several burgundy leather-bound ledgers from the cabinet and set them in a pile on the desk.

Seated next to his friend, he set to work on their task.

No stone could be left unturned.

Not one.

Chapter 6

Under a patchy gray sky with a peek of blue trying to push through, Sophia gripped the edge of the small carriage window as the horses trotted up the promenade to the grand entrance of Montagu House. Together, the four ladies alighted before the British Museum and strolled across the courtyard, Sawyer and Gorman one step behind them. The museum's main façade held seventeen bays with a prominent three bay center and three bay ends, which bordered the service wings. Sitting two stories high with a basement and a protruding mansard roof, Montagu House held a regal and elegant dome over the center. So stunning, and of clear French design. The museum was sophisticated and stately with an open field at the rear and extensive gardens all around, which visitors to the museum could enjoy at their leisure.

Sophia entered the front door of the building and as she did each time she arrived in this most wondrous of places, halted to admire the sheer beauty of the main floor's immense interior. Groups of visitors mingled before paintings and exhibits, all here enjoying a day immersing themselves in all the museum had to offer. A wide staircase wound around the side of the central saloon and swept upward to the next floor, where high latticed windows at the front of the house allowed light to stream in. A high ceiling rose overhead with painted artwork gracing its entirety—a stunning centerpiece.

"Oh, look at these beautiful murals on the walls." Maria gasped as she caught sight of the featured paintings to their left, the murals on show painted by both Italian and French artists.

"Let's admire those first." This was Maria's day and she'd do all she could to ensure her friend enjoyed herself. Drawing Maria along, she perused paintings both donated to the museum, and purchased by the trustees to ensure the fine pieces wouldn't be lost to the public.

An hour later, they finally ascended the stairs, which in itself took time as one couldn't simply wander past each high window along the stairway without halting to admire the extensive view of the gardens spread outside.

At the top, they wandered underneath an elegant arch framing a double doorway and into the first of dozens of upper rooms. Each well-crafted display caught their attention and they admired table after table.

Captain James Cook's exhibit took Sophia's breath away. So many pieces were on display from his travels across the South Seas, each item giving a glimpse into previously unknown lands. Next to her, Ellie smoothed one hand over an animal skin and read the documented entry about it to them. Olivia marveled over the pieces of rock, sculpted marble and ornamentation from the islands which Cook had discovered within waters that had never been chartered before. Across from her, Maria gushed over the well-handcrafted pieces gifted to Cook from several island chiefs who spoke in languages unknown.

Goodness, but their world was so vast, far greater than Sophia had ever believed it could be. How incredible to undertake such an adventure. She trailed one finger along a piece of the foremast of Cook's ship, *HMS Resolution*, which had been damaged by the rough seas after he'd left the Hawaiian Islands.

She stood quietly, reverently, as she read the plaque detailing Cook's unfortunate demise. After leaving Hawaii, Captain Cook's expedition of 1779 had been forced to return to the islands after only a week at sea. As they arrived where they'd been greeted with great respect only a few days past, this time they were set upon by the natives for reasons unknown to them, although they suspected it had to do with the islanders' beliefs and the gods they worshipped. Only a few of his men managed to escape to the safety of Cook's two ships, although Cook himself was killed by a mob of islanders, his body taken by the Hawaiians for ritualistic burial purposes, although some of his remains were returned to his crew and once they had been, his men set sail after repairing their vessel, then officially buried Cook at sea, within the waters he'd cherished exploring.

Cook's life had come to such an abrupt and sad end.

Dipping her head with respect, she stepped away and followed Maria and her sisters, who'd already continued on.

Maria and Olivia halted before a marble statue, Sawyer remaining close to Maria.

Ellie perused a series of oil paintings next, Gorman keeping an eye on her.

Sophia smiled and veered toward an enticing collection of books. She'd always adored the written word and she took her time thumbing through the volumes, some tomes Winterly actually had on his study shelves.

At the table next to her, a man wearing a beaver hat stood with the rim of his hat shading the top half of his dark head. With the collar of his jacket flicked high and hiding the lower half of his face, he appeared mysterious. He picked up an engraved gem, set it down and perused the coins and prints which he seemed to find of great interest, then suddenly he tipped his gaze toward her. Brilliant sapphire eyes sparkled, his jaw firmly set, the way he stood both elusive and regal.

"My apologies." Cheeks flaming, she turned her gaze back on the tomes. Never had she been caught staring so openly at a man.

"Apology accepted." He smiled, his lips lifting, his blue eyes brightening even further. "Would you be Lady Sophia Trentbury, by chance?"

"Ah, yes." Baffled, she frowned. "I'm sorry, but do I know you?"

"No, although we share two acquaintances, one being the Earl of Donnelly, the other the Duke of Ashten, your sister's husband." He stuck one hand in his inner jacket pocket and removed a piece of thick parchment. Unfolding it, he continued in a low murmur, "Donnelly handed this drawing to me earlier this morning. You will of course be aware of it since you're the lady who discovered it in the earl's library. He has informed me about what happened, of course."

"Oh, you must be Captain Bourbon." Her heartbeat raced. "You're aiding the earl in his investigations?"

"Yes, and I hope I'm not being too forward in introducing myself."

"We don't exactly have someone here to perform an introduction for us." She also wished to speak to this gentleman. A quick glance about as she checked to ensure no one paid too much attention to them, and since her sisters and Maria were still immersed in other displays, she faced the man again. "We shall introduce ourselves. I'm Lady Sophia, the Earl of Winterly's sister."

"It's a pleasure to meet you, Lady Sophia." Drawing tucked away, he caught her gloved hand and pressed a kiss to her knuckles. "I have something to show you, an item from the treasure chest which I've spoken to Donnelly and Ashten about." He removed a piece of jade from his inside coat pocket and carefully held the treasure toward her. "This is the actual jade mask portrayed in the drawing you found."

"Oh my, how did you come by it?" She held the mask carefully in her hands, the piece's mouth and eye sockets open and carved with an exquisite eye for detail. By a master carver for certain. Shaking at the immense find she now held, she murmured, "This mask is beautiful, extremely beautiful."

"Priceless too."

"Yes, I imagine that is so." She handed the mask back, which he accepted and returned to his pocket.

"I would like to speak to you further, in private if I may?" Extending one crooked elbow, he continued,

"Would you take a short walk with me, into the next room?"

"Of course." Somewhat dazed, she accepted his offered arm and he guided her into the side room where two people stood admiring an exhibit along the far wall. "What did you wish to speak to me about, Captain Bourbon?"

"The sunken treasure chest. I've learnt it doesn't belong to the Spanish, but to the Portuguese House of Braganza."

"It does?"

"Yes, and as I've informed Donnelly and Ashten, two and a half years past, when the entire Braganza Dynasty of Portugal fled into exile, the treasure within the chest was left behind with the Spanish royal family, of which the Spanish promised to send the chest along when all became safe. The ceremonial mask I've shown you was recovered in the early hours of this morning from the town office of Mr. Blackburne, a wealthy solicitor. He bought the piece for a large sum from a contact of his at the eastern docks. I've yet to uncover who that contact is, but I shall. It's only a matter of time until I discover exactly who stole the chest, but I can only do so with your aid."

"How so?"

He looked into her eyes. "My lady, I captain a vessel called The Cobra, which goes by the same name as my gaming hell, and a year ago I sailed into Algiers and while there visited a wise woman who is very dear to me. Her name is Shira Ria, *la maga,* or as some would say, the sorceress. Shira is known to read the palm of your hand, or offer you one of her special coffees and read the remains she spills onto a saucer. She is a foreseer, whom I've mentioned to Donnelly and Ashten."

"How intriguing." Captivated, she couldn't look away. "Did she read your future?"

"Yes, although not only mine, but yours as well."

"I don't understand."

"Shira told me of my past, my present, and my future." His words were soft, gentle, reverent. "She informed me that one day I would meet two ladies, all in regard to a drawing and certain events that would unfold with stolen treasure. The name of the first lady would be Sophia, the name of the second, Olivia, which of course is your name and that of your sister."

"How incredible. Please, tell me more."

"Shira told me that you would need my aid, in a matter of the heart."

"Indeed, I do." She couldn't deny that, not when Donnelly held her heart.

"Shira also shared with me that the lady who found the drawing would not be aware of all she knew, that I'm to keep her close until all is unraveled, that throughout the days ahead I shall be her guardian. My duty will be to keep you safe."

"What of Olivia?" She fluttered a hand over her heart.

"The lady named Olivia would one day offer me an olive branch, the symbol of peace."

"Olivia's name is derived from the olive branch."

"Shira insisted Olivia would one day be my saving grace, an angel sent to me at a time when I would need one the most." He set a hand at her back and steered her to the next display. "One doesn't take Shira's words lightly, and so I must ask that you turn to me whenever you have need of aid. Send me word to my gaming hell and I shall come when you call."

"What else did Shira say?" Deep intrigue pulsed within her. She would dearly love to meet this foreseer.

"She issued a grave warning, one I'd best not share as yet. When the time comes, I shall though. For now, I would like you to use my given name. Please, call me Anteros, if that is not being too forward of me to ask?"

"Very forward, but these are unusual circumstances, so yes, I shall call you Anteros, provided you call me Sophia." Goodness, they hadn't been introduced formally and now they'd invited each other to use their given names. Mama would be shocked at her behavior, although Mama had also said just this morning that one couldn't live their life in fear, which she intended to take directly to heart.

She walked with Anteros into yet another side room toward a new display, one showcasing a lifelike series of large sculptures, one ironically of Anteros, the Greek god of love and passion. Wings sprouted from the statue's back, a cloth draped over the sculpture's shoulder and around his lower body, his chest exposed and muscles flexed as he held a bow with an arrow on the verge of being released. Another couple admired the statue, their heads bent together as they spoke in low tones. "It appears there is another Anteros in the room," she whispered to Anteros.

"Yes, which is a clear sign that you and I are where we should currently be."

"How did you come by the name Anteros?"

"My mother had a huge fascination for all things Roman and Greek, particularly surrounding the gods." He glanced over the top of her head, one brow lifting as Olivia wandered into the room, her sister searching for her.

She waved out and Olivia hurried across.

Under his breath, Anteros murmured, "Ah, *bello*. My angel has fire in her eyes and purpose in her stride. Sophia, I beg of you an introduction."

Olivia halted before them, worry clear to see in her eyes. "Is everything all right, Sophia? Sawyer informed me that someone might be detaining you."

"Not detaining," she corrected. "I've been enjoying a delightful conversation with—well—Olivia, allow me to introduce you to Captain Anteros Bourbon. Captain, this is my younger sister, Lady Olivia Trentbury."

The captain removed his hat and tucked it under one arm, his black hair shimmering a vibrant blue on the ends, the color an exact match to his blue eyes. "*Piacere*. It's a pleasure to meet you, Lady Olivia." Bourbon lifted her sister's gloved hand to his lips and kissed her knuckles. "This is a meeting I have both longed for and feared."

"Bourbon? As in the man my sister has spoken of, the spymaster aiding the Earl of Donnelly in his investigations?"

"Yes, that is exactly who I am."

"Oh, well, it is a pleasure to meet you. A surprise, but still a pleasure." Olivia stepped closer to Bourbon, her voice hushed so it didn't travel any farther than the three of them. "Have you made any progress with your investigations?"

"I have, and will continue to do so." Bourbon's voice became a low drawl and Olivia stared at her hand still in his and dropped it quickly to her side.

"My apologies. Pardon me." Olivia pinched her lips together.

"You are pardoned." A teasing smile from the captain as he stuck his hat back on his head and straightened to his towering height. "Ladies, I do believe luncheon is being served in the tearoom. Would you allow me to escort you both there?"

Since Sophia wished to learn more about Donnelly's mysterious spymaster, she nodded enthusiastically. "Kind sir, we'd be honored."

"Wonderful." He extended crooked elbows to both her and Olivia. "Except the honor is all mine. I can assure you of that."

Chapter 7

That night as a thick fog settled over his house, Donnelly strode back and forth under the front eaves as he awaited Maria's return from the museum, his chest tight as wispy streaks of mist swirled all about. Ten o'clock. Maria should have been home hours ago. They'd agreed to eat at eight and she'd never been late to a meal in the past. Perhaps he shouldn't have allowed her to leave the house, or at least not for the entire day, and why hadn't Sawyer sent word to him if they'd been delayed for some reason?

The clatter of horses' hooves and carriage wheels finally broke the stillness and he bounded down the front pathway as Winterly's coach appeared out of the misty darkness. The conveyance rocked to a stop and Sawyer, cloaked head to toe in black, bounded down from next to the driver.

"All is well, my lord." Sawyer set the step on the ground and opened the door. "We suffered not one broken wheel, but unfortunately two. Ten dratted minutes apart as well."

"Maria?" He held out a hand as his sister appeared at

the carriage door. As soon as she set her fingers in his, he smothered his sister in his arms, her dark cloak swaying from her shoulders. "I've been incredibly worried."

"I'm so sorry. I couldn't send word about our delay, not when the ladies and I had to wait for the coachman to effect repairs and Sawyer wished to remain with me. I then insisted they be dropped off first since we had to pass right by Blackgale House and Winterly's town residence on our way here." Eyes bright, she kissed his cheek. "I've had a wonderful day and wish to tell you all about it. Have you eaten?"

"No, but we shall once we're inside." He closed the door and called out to the liveried driver, "Take care as you return. The fog is thick."

"I shall, my lord." The driver bobbed his head and cracked his whip.

Winterly's coach rattled back into the soupy mist, the fog swallowing it whole.

He offered Maria his arm and guided her into the house.

"I'll freshen up and be with you shortly." With a twiddle of her fingers, she hurried up the stairs.

As she disappeared around the corner of the upper landing, he faced Sawyer who remained standing at attention next to the front door. "I'd like a full report."

"Lady Maria toured most of the museum and enjoyed herself immensely. She and the other ladies even took luncheon together in the tearoom overlooking the rear gardens of Montagu House. I do need to inform you though that a gentleman joined them for the midday meal." His man cleared his throat, a frown furrowing his brow.

"Captain Bourbon."

Shock pulsed through him. None of the ladies had met Bourbon, of which an introduction would have been needed. Certainly, Ellie, as the Duchess of Ashten, would have been considered a suitable chaperone for the other three younger ladies, but still, a fierce need to protect their reputations throbbed through him. "Continue," he muttered.

"The captain remained with the ladies for the entire afternoon before stationing another man to maintain a guard over them when he left, very discreetly of course. The ladies weren't aware, although I noticed the man immediately. I had a word with him, Giovani, the captain's right-hand man, who I've actually spoken to when passing your messages along to Bourbon at his gaming hell."

"Interesting." After his meeting with Bourbon at his warehouse, the spymaster had traveled to the museum and sought out Sophia. He had no desire to bring Sophia any further into his current investigations, which he'd have to make clear to Bourbon. He nodded at Sawyer. "I'll sort everything out. For now, I want you to rest for a couple of hours, then take over from Rignor at the docks. Report back to me if anything of interest arises."

He'd had a man positioned on watch near his warehouses since his return a week past. Nothing unusual had been noted, but maintaining observant eyes and ears along the docks was all important.

"Of course, my lord." Sawyer dipped his head and closed the front door behind him as he left.

"Oh, I'm absolutely famished." Maria descended the stairs in fresh clothes, a dark skirt and white blouse, her veil removed and her brown locks released from her chignon and now bouncing down her back. She swished in beside him, linked her arm with his and beamed. "You look famished as well."

"I'm starved, but more so for your company than anything else." He led his sister into the dining room, seated her then took his place at the head of the table. Candles glowed from the chandelier overhead, the table set with sparkling cutlery and glasses. The servants set their meals before them, filled their wine glasses then quietly left the room. Once gone, he raised his glass to his sister. "To museums and dear friends."

"Yes, to museums and dear friends." After a clink of her glass to his, she sipped her wine. "Did Sawyer mention that Captain Bourbon joined us for luncheon?"

"He did."

"Goodness, but he's such an interesting man. I did wonder if I would ever get the chance to meet your spymaster. I'm glad I have."

"How did he introduce himself?"

"Oh, ah, when I met him, he'd already spoken at length to Sophia and she introduced him to Olivia then Ellie and me. I can only surmise he'd already met Sophia." She cut into her roast beef and gravy. "Mmm, delicious," she murmured around a mouthful then continued, "Did you know that the captain has traveled extensively throughout the Americas?"

"Where exactly did he say he'd been?" His sister might have actually learnt more about Bourbon today than he had. He chewed his meat, intent on hearing everything.

"He spoke of Jamaica where Uncle John is stationed." She forked roasted parsnips and carrots glistening with butter. "He told us some rousing stories."

"Do tell." He ate another bite as she broke into a smile.

"One story in particular which had us all captivated was when he was at sea on his ship. He discovered a vessel flying France's colors approaching him at full speed, and when he trained his telescope on the ship, not one Frenchman stood on board. Instead pirates had taken the French warship over. The pirates then fired their cannons at Bourbon's ship, and he decided his best course of action was to attempt to fool them. He trimmed the sails and allowed the blackguards to toss their grappling hooks over the side of his vessel, then when the pirates boarded, his men attacked and successfully brought the scoundrels to their knees."

"That sounds like a winning battle indeed."

"Yes, and Bourbon commandeered the stolen warship for himself and added it to his own fleet. We cheered at that news. The less ships Napoleon has at sea, the better, and Bourbon admitted that he'd gotten quite adept at seizing Napoleon's ships when they strayed too close to his own."

"Well, provided he's intent on capturing warships from France, he'll remain a friend of mine."

"My thoughts exactly." Maria bubbled with excitement. "I thoroughly enjoyed viewing all the exhibits today, as well as having the company of the ladies and their spirited conversation. I've missed being among my dear friends."

"You certainly look happier than I've seen you in a long time." He owed Sophia his immense thanks for bringing back the wide smile on his sister's face. Gently, he cupped Maria's cheek, his heart squeezing tight. "You're returning to the world, and it does my heart good to see."

"You look happier today as well, worried of course when I first rode in, but more yourself this morning at the breakfast table, and tonight while we've been eating."

"I am making leeway in my investigations, moving ahead one step at a time."

"That is good news." She stifled a yawn. "Oh, my apologies, the day is catching up on me. How was your search of Father's office at the warehouse?"

"Ashten and I perused every single burgundy ledger which Mr. Taylor gave Father these past seven years. Nothing seemed amiss, although I spoke to Bourbon at the warehouse before he joined you at the museum. He has recovered one of the artifacts from the chest, the jade mask, which was a match to the drawing Sophia uncovered in the library. He's making good progress in his investigations."

"That's wonderful to hear." She patted her mouth, a yawn this time escaping.

"You're clearly exhausted. Retire for the night if you wish. We can speak again in the morning when we break our fast."

"I'm certainly tired." Setting her napkin on the table and positioning her cutlery on her plate so the staff would know she was done, she rose and hugged him tight. "Good night, my dear brother. I love you."

"As I love you." He didn't wish to release her, but grudgingly he did. "Rest well."

"I certainly shall. Rest well yourself." She swished from the room.

He wouldn't be able to, not when he had so many questions rolling around in his head. What had Sophia and

Bourbon chatted about? He also wished to ascertain she was well. He couldn't imagine the spymaster distressing her in any way, but he would check on her all the same.

He left the table, collected his greatcoat and hat from his butler then slipped outside and joined Parker in the stables. At his request, his groomsman readied his stallion for him and once he had, he mounted and rode hard through the dark, foggy streets toward Sophia's home.

Slowing his horse and trotting in behind thick bushes bordering Winterly's townhouse, he remained hidden atop his mount. The lights along the lower floor blinked out one by one, and he searched the upper level and counted the windows until he reached Sophia's bedchamber. A gentle light lit her closed red-gold drapes. The hour was exceedingly late, too late to knock upon their front door.

He'd knock upon her window instead.

A quick dismount.

He looped the reins of his horse to the low branch of the nearby oak tree, scooped a few fallen acorns from the grass and snuck through the thick foliage around the side of the house. As he did, he made certain no one else lurked about, then once assured he was alone, halted underneath her window. A swing as he lobbed an acorn at her window. *Tap.* Another acorn. *Tap.*

All remained quiet above.

No, he wouldn't be deterred.

Three more acorns. *Tap, tap, tap.*

Her drapes swayed, and she lifted her window with nary a noise.

She stuck her head out and frowned at him, her golden locks loose and mussed about her shoulders. "Good grief is that you, James?"

"Yes, indeed it is." He kept his voice low, one finger to his mouth. "Shh, I don't want to wake anyone."

"What on earth are you doing here in the middle of the night?" she whispered in a mad rush then gasped, one hand clutched to her chest. "Is Maria all right?"

"Yes, she's fine. She also thoroughly enjoyed her day with you and your sisters. I wish to thank you," he whispered back, "for entertaining her as you did."

"There's no need to thank me." An annoyed huff. "She's my friend. I would do anything for her, for you too if you allowed it."

"Anything?"

"Yes."

"Perfect." He pointed around the other side of the house. "I want you to sneak downstairs to the side door. I'll meet you at the servants' entrance."

"Pardon?" Her mouth formed a perfect O.

"You heard me."

"I did, but—no, never mind. Give me two minutes." She disappeared, her curtains swishing back together.

A grin slashed his face and he sent a quick prayer skyward that she was indeed sneaking downstairs this very instant to see him.

Keeping to the shadows of the house, he crept to the side door where household deliveries were made and waited on the doorstep.

Less than two minutes later, the door opened and Sophia stood there in her ivory nightgown with her bare toes peeking out from under the hem, her cheeks flushed and blue eyes bright.

His heartbeat thundered in his ears, his need to hold her now raging strongly through him. This might have been a bad idea, asking her to let him in, but he wouldn't back down now. He needed to know what she and Bourbon had discussed, or at least that's what he'd told himself countless times on his ride here. He stepped inside and closed the door. "Lead the way to your bedchamber."

Without a word, she caught his hand and tugged him through the kitchen then up the darkened servants' stairwell. At the bend in the stairs, they passed a single lamp burning in a wall sconce behind a glass casing. Onward, she hurried and at the top, tightened her grip on his hand and rushed along the upper landing. In her room, she released his fingers, closed the door with barely a snick and leaned back against it. "Right, you are now here, in my bedchamber, as requested. I can't believe you came to see me."

"I had no choice." A log burned in her fireplace, the flames casting a flickering glow over the sheer golden canopy sweeping around her four-poster bed, her bedcovers all rumpled and Marco Polo's book open on her nightstand.

"Something dire must have happened for you to ask me to sneak you inside, but I'm afraid to ask what it might be." She stuck her thumb in her mouth and nibbled adoringly on the end, her gaze searching his. "You're certain Maria is all right?"

"Yes, and I came because I'm worried about you." He curled one hand around her waist and—hell, she had such soft curves under the thin ivory cotton. He groaned, bliss pulsing through him, his cock hardening and breeches tightening. "I needed to assure myself you were well. Maria told me about Captain Bourbon joining you at the museum. What exactly did he speak to you about?"

She stood unmoving, silent and watchful.

"Sophia?" He was so physically aware of her, of how each of her breaths made her nightgown cling more deliciously to her breasts. Gently, he pressed a kiss to her temple and her breath whooshed out. He was dangerously tempted to tip her head back and steal a deeply passionate kiss from her, to plunder her mouth and never let her go. Instead, he remained right where he was, breathing far too raggedly. "What did you and Bourbon discuss?"

"We spoke of many things, that the chest actually belongs to the Portuguese House of Braganza, and—" Her brow puckered. "Well, as strange as it may sound, a foreseer told him he would one day meet me, that I'd need his aid. She instructed him to keep me close."

"He mentioned a foreseer to me this morning as well."

"Is that why you're here?" She swayed into him, their bodies brushing each other's. "To ask me about Anteros?"

"Anteros? You're calling him by his given name?"

"Yes, it seemed only right since we'll be spending time together."

"I don't want you spending any time with him."

"You don't have a say in the matter, unless you've changed your mind about staking a claim on me." She lifted her chin, in that defiant way which he both adored and detested.

"No, that I'll never do."

"Then I'll spend time with him as I please."

"There is passion between us. You can't deny it."

"Which is what I told you in your library." She

grumbled under her breath. "I won't allow you to use my own words against me. Clearly, you're still rather randy."

"Terribly so." He swept in and kissed her, one deeply needful kiss he couldn't halt or control.

"James." She clutched ahold of his lapels. "Cease your jealousy. There is only one man I desire, and that man is you."

"I want you, but I can't have you," he whispered against her lips. "Not while death and danger darkens my door."

"What if we could set aside all that has happened? What if the war never raged, if there was never a need for you to join the hussars, if a murderer hadn't stolen the lives of your loved ones, if love and peace prevailed?" Her gaze pleaded with his. "Tell me we'd be together."

"We would be together," he admitted. "Although all those things have happened, and I can't keep you completely and utterly safe unless I keep you far away from me."

"Yet here you are, still wanting me the same way I want you." Her blue eyes softened, a smile lighting them from within. "I hope you don't think me a hoyden, but there is a bed only a few steps away, and I'd like you to stay with me so we can talk."

"The last thing I want to do right now is talk." Looking deep into her eyes, he removed his greatcoat and tossed it and his hat onto her corner floral armchair. "I shouldn't have ridden here tonight. All I'm doing is drawing you deeper into the chaos surrounding me."

"If you don't want to talk, then what do you want to do?" Her eyelashes swept down to her high cheeks then back up again, her soft murmur that of a siren's whisper. "Make you mine, Sophia."

Chapter 8

"I'm already yours, James."

Sophia spread one hand over his chest, her heartbeat pounding against her ribcage.

"If anything happened to you because I didn't take enough care with your safety, then I'd gladly slit my own throat so you remained out of harm's way." He wound a long lock of her golden hair around his fist and kept her imprisoned against him.

"I'm safe right now." Her head spun, both from his immense closeness and the headiness of his powerful touch. "Stake your claim."

"You truly wish for me to do so?"

"Yes." He'd kissed her only moments ago and sent her mind spinning, her desire flaring. She certainly understood he wouldn't be able to make a formal offer for her, but if he made her a promise from his heart which she could hold onto, then doing so would be just as powerful. Slowly, she eased his jacket from his shoulders and let the fabric slide to the floor where it crumpled into a heap. No faltering. She would show him with her actions exactly how much she loved him. She unknotted his cravat, tossed it aside then flicked his shirt buttons open before smoothing over the hard muscles of his abdomen, his torso strong and rigidly firm. On her toes, she touched her mouth to his, her fingers digging into his muscled flesh.

"You will be the end of me. I'm certain of it." Groaning, he caught her head in his hands and took their kiss deeper, longer, an entwining of their very souls. "I want to devour you, Sophia, but I won't ruin you."

"Devouring sounds delicious."

"You need to cease encouraging me." He nudged her backward, not toward the bed, but until her back came up against the wall, the rigid lines crossing his belly tightening so magnificently.

"I trust you." She'd given him her trust the first day they'd met, when he'd caught her as she'd toppled from a wooden pail while trying to rescue a wee kitten from its precarious perch between two branches. Never would she take that trust back.

"Then let me show you the woman I see before me, the one I wish to stake my claim of, the one I shall always adore." He loosened the laces at the neckline of her nightgown and slid the fabric down her arms. The ivory linen caught at her elbows, her breasts spilling free, then gently, he turned her to face the tall-standing oval mirror propped in one corner.

Her reflection shimmered back at her. She stood bared to her waist, the man at her back shirtless and a head taller than her, the light from the glowing fire glittering in his passion-filled eyes. He trailed a finger along the arch of her brow down to the sweeping hollow of her cheek then along her jaw. She tingled everywhere he touched.

"You've skin as pale as alabaster and as soft as satin." A sweep of his hand down her neck, his voice low and husky, his gaze moving over her breasts. "You're so beautiful."

Her skin heated, her cheeks flushing, her nipples hardening into tight peaks. She'd bathed in a tub in this very spot, the fire roaring, and countless times she'd stepped clear of that tub and dressed before her mirror. She'd seen her body, each and every curve, but with his gaze upon her, she saw herself differently for the first time in her life.

She saw herself as a woman being looked upon by a man.

She saw what he saw.

Desire. Need. Love. All shining in her eyes.

She tipped her head to the side and rested it back against his shoulder, her back arched and breasts pressing forward.

James dipped his head to her neck, his dark hair sweeping forward over his brow.

She gasped as he nuzzled her flesh, as he lifted his hands and cupped her breasts.

"I want to bring you pleasure, my sweet Sophia." Nibbling on her earlobe, he kneaded her breasts. "Will you allow it?"

"Yes, by all means, please continue." So many sensations roared through her, all she desperately desired.

"I want to suck on your breasts." He grinned wickedly as he stepped around in front of her. "Does that request shock you?"

"Yes." Heat throbbed between her legs. "But in a good way."

"I want to lavish attention on you." Head bent, he wrapped his mouth around her nipple while he gently pinched the other.

As he took the tender tip deeper into his mouth, his dark head an alluring contrast against her pale skin, she gripped his shoulders and held on tight.

"My sweet, this is why ladies are never permitted to be alone with a man." He licked across to her other breast, his tongue tracing the heart-shaped mole above her heart as he did. Tingles raced across her skin, from the top of her head to the tips of her toes.

More sucking, so deeply delicious.

She melted, although all too soon he swept back around to her back, his gaze once more on hers in the mirror, his gaze burning with desire. "I need to see you fall apart in my arms. Say yes, that I might have my wicked way with you."

"Yes." No hesitation. She wanted everything he could give her.

"Thank you." He pushed her nightgown past her elbows and the cotton slithered to the floor, leaving her completely bared to his gaze.

She squeezed her eyes shut, shock and desire pulsing through her in equal waves.

"If you want me to stop, simply say so."

"No, if you stop, I shall never speak to you again." She opened her eyes and peeked at her reflection. Longs legs, curved hips, and golden curls covered her entrance below, his gaze moving over all of her.

"You're such a vixen, my vixen." He swept his fingers along her inner thigh and gently nudged her legs farther apart. With soft butterfly nips, he trailed his lips across her collarbone and into the sensitive curve where her shoulder and neck met.

Anticipation thrummed through her.

Being held in his arms was spellbinding.

He pressed his palm flat to her belly then speared his fingers downward into her curls. One finger dipped between her folds and nestled there. She held her breath and leaned back against him, then when he rubbed her nub, she gasped, her legs trembling.

She'd touched herself there before while bathing, had found the spot sweetly sensitive, but with him touching her in the same spot, everything was different. She gripped his outer thighs through his buff breeches as something devilishly hard prodded her lower back. "Can I touch you?" she whispered. "The same way you're touching me?"

"No, otherwise I'll come in my breeches. I'm already extremely close to doing so and I won't allow that. Your pleasure comes first."

"How does a man come?" She couldn't help but ask the question, particularly when she wanted no secrets between them. "Will you tell me?"

"A man, when he reaches the pinnacle of his passion"—he pushed his hips firmer into her back, the bulge somehow even larger—"comes by way of release, ejaculating semen from his cock. It's a thick whitish substance and should I release that inside of you, it could leave you with child, which would cause you ruin, and which I will never do."

"I see."

"But you can come at my hand, and find pleasure." He plunged his finger deep inside her channel.

"Oh my." She closed her eyes as sheer pleasure stormed through her.

He sucked on her earlobe, his fingers rubbing inside her lower flesh.

Never had she experienced such heavenly heights as this. She moaned, and he stroked her harder and faster. So deliciously fast. Everything went dark and her core sparked and caught alight. A fire of desire roared through her and she soared clear of her body, catapulting to the very stars. Dizzy, her legs buckled and—

"I've got you." He caught her up in his arms and carefully laid her on her bed. With his boots kicked off, he unbuttoned the front of his breeches. Standing beside her bed, he held his handkerchief over his freed cock and pumped himself in long pulls.

"Kiss me," she whispered, needing him closer.

"I can't, or else I'll toss this cloth and push my cock inside you. I want to, Sophia, more than I could ever express with words." He increased his speed, his breath coming more rapidly, then he gritted his teeth, his body convulsing. Growling low, he jerked and leaned over her. He pressed his forehead to her forehead, his handkerchief wet with his seed. "Giving you up, will never be an option, not anymore. As soon as I've completed my investigations and sorted out this mess surrounding me, I will make you my wife. Say yes, that you'll wait for me, for however long it takes."

"Yes, I'll wait for you, for forever long it takes." She

wrapped her arms around his neck and tugged him down onto her. She kissed his jaw, his ear, his bare shoulder. "I love you, James."

"I love you too." He swept a lock of her hair behind her ear then kissed her with an open-mouthed kiss that had her clinging to him with breathy moans.

"You looked so stunning when you came. I shall never forget that moment, not for the rest of my days." He lifted up a touch, fastened his breeches then settled back over top of her. "One of us needs to remain at least partially clothed, and that shall be me.

"I shan't forget the moment you came either." She tickled her fingers over his bare chest, then down each indent lining his belly, his midsection packed with muscle. "I love touching you. I fear I'm becoming a wanton woman."

"You can be as wanton as you like with me." He rolled them both over until she came up on top of him, her breasts pressing into his chest. With one arm curved around her waist, he settled his other hand over one lower cheek and stroked a small circle with his thumb across her skin.

White-hot flames danced back to life within her. "You took me to a place far beyond my own body." She trailed a finger along his lush lower lip. "I adored it."

"You are learning how to be a seductress rather quickly." He gripped her hips, lifted her bodily higher and fastened his mouth over one nipple. "Which I love," he muttered as he swept to her other nipple and sucked that one deep between his lips.

"My lord, I do agree with the way you stake your claim."

"I believe I agree with it far more."

He crushed her in his arms and kissed her wildly, as if trying to take her into his very heart and soul, which he already had. Never did she wish to be anywhere else.

Chapter 9

A few hours later, not long before dawn, Donnelly had to force himself to pull Sophia's nightgown over her luscious body and leave her bed. He grumbled as he donned his shirt over his breeches, knotted his cravat and buttoned his jacket, all while she smiled with her head on her pillow and her golden locks in complete disarray. "Do we have an understanding?" he asked her from the side table where he'd secured a piece of paper from the top drawer and dipped her quill into the ink bottle.

"What understanding would that be?" Such a sultry smile as she pushed her elbow into the mattress and settled her head in her upturned palm.

"That Bourbon and I will be doing our damnedest to hunt down the thief and killer, and that once justice has been served, then I can return to claim you as my wife."

"Oh, we most certainly have that understanding." Her blue eyes twinkled with devilish merriment.

"Good." He scrawled across the paper, the comfort of writing to her as he did each morning instilling some calm in him before he had to leave her.

My dearest Sophia,

Last night you came apart in my arms and being the cad I am, I wish only to return to you each night henceforth, so I might pleasure you again in every possible way there is to pleasure a woman. Clearly, I can no longer refrain from taking liberties with you, not when you bewitch me at every turn. That said, you must not answer my call again should I toss acorns at your window. I beg this of you, otherwise I shall be placing your life in danger when that is something I have no intention of ever doing. Give me the time I need to track down the killer. That is all I'm asking.

Yours with complete devotion,
James.

"What are you writing?" Her questioning words were slightly slurred, her need for sleep clear to hear. Not surprising. He hadn't allowed her any rest since he'd arrived.

"A letter, which you must read, then I shall take it with me." Such an incriminating note couldn't remain where one of her household might stumble upon it. No, when he arrived home, he would add it to his locked box of letters.

Returning to her side, he handed her the missive and stood waiting with his hands clasped behind his back and hopefully a stern expression on his face.

"All right. I shall read it." A plump of her pillows as she rested her back against them. With the parchment in hand, she read, a frown slowly taking away her smile. Carefully, she folded the paper in three and handed it back to him, her frown remaining in place. "All I've read is completely understandable."

"Thank you. Agreeing to my request is incredibly important." He slotted the letter into his inner jacket pocket.

"James, I said understandable, not that I'm in full agreement. Every day you are left wondering who killed your father and brother, if perhaps you're their next target, but you shouldn't cease living your life. I can't possibly turn you away should you toss acorns at my window."

"I will never allow any harm to come to you."

"There are so many men, women, and children dying due to this dratted war. For goodness' sake, women wed and can perish in childbirth. Does that mean those women should never lie with their husbands? If one doesn't look where one walks, they might step into the path of a carriage. Does that mean we should never leave our homes?" She shuffled onto her knees, her nightgown pulling against her front then she rose up onto her feet and eyed him nose to nose. "Life isn't set in stone, so one must take happiness where one can get it. You bring me happiness. I will take that at every possible opportunity."

"It is also the right of any man to ensure the protection of his family."

"I'm not yet your family." She jabbed a finger into his chest. "Before my papa passed away, he told me that one should always fight for what is right in our world and to never give up on those we cherish. I finally understand exactly what he meant. Even though you don't wish for my aid in your current battle, I must offer it all the same. Everything within me demands it."

"I have buried my father and brother, well before they should have ever gone to their graves. I won't bury you as well." He palmed her nape and drew her mouth to his. He kissed her, with all the desire and fury swelling deep within him. "I want to make you my wife, Sophia, and I will, but I need more time. That's all I'm asking for. Remain where you'll be safe until I claim you fully, with all that I am."

"My heart ceases to beat when you kiss me." She clung to him. "I can't lose you."

"I can't lose you either."

"I don't like that you're leaving." She caught her breath and pressed a hand to his heart, her fingers firm over his chest.

"I must leave. Daylight looms." He firmed his resolve and stepped away from her. He opened the door, his heart squeezing tight. The last thing he wanted to do was leave her, only he had no other choice.

"Wait, James. Let me check that all remains clear." She snuck off her bed, eased past him and peeked into the darkened hallway, then with a nod, gripped his hand and escorted him downstairs the same way they'd traversed up.

He allowed it, needing these last few moments with her.

At the side entrance near the kitchens, he slipped on his greatcoat and stuffed his hat on his head. No more could he delay. The skies were lightening, dawn so terribly close.

"I need you to send word to me that you've arrived home safely." She wrapped her arms around his waist and rested her cheek on his chest. "I will continue to worry otherwise."

"Of course." He didn't wish to leave her worrying

about him unnecessarily. Gently, he tipped her face to his, caught her mouth and kissed her until he'd hopefully muddled her thoughts. He'd certainly muddled his own.

Giving his head a shake, he stepped back and after soaking in the sight of her one last time, ducked through the nippy drizzle, the fog still as thick as it had been on his journey here last night. He unknotted his stallion's reins, mounted his steed and thrust his knees into his horse's flanks. Spurring his horse onward, he rode home swiftly and arrived as the dawn sun breached the horizon.

One leg swung over, he dismounted and thumped to the gravelly ground before handing his reins to his stable hand who raced forward.

"My lord!" Sawyer galloped in and bounded from his saddle, soot smeared across his chin and hands.

"What's happened?" His footman would never have left his post at the docks, not until he'd sent a man to take his place, not unless an emergency had arisen.

"The Fortune Maria has returned from her latest voyage, without Captain Lewiston on board." Half bent over, his hands clasped to his knees, he dragged in a staggered breath from his fast ride. "The ship's first mate informed me that the captain made port farther along the river twenty-four hours ago. He wished to visit his brother, Geoffrey Lewiston, who owns the Boar Head Tavern, although the captain promised he wouldn't be long. Unfortunately, he never returned and the first mate sent Paddy, the cabin boy, to seek out the captain. The lad disappeared and since the Fortune Maria had no permission to maintain the mooring at the eastern docks, the officer continued on along the Thames. Mr. Taylor is now overseeing the removal of the ship's cargo into your warehouses."

Mr. Taylor would ensure a smooth transition of the cargo. That he had no doubt about. Hmm, only what to do about Captain Lewiston? Lewiston had visited his brother, Geoffrey, from time to time in the past, but he was never gone for long, and for the cabin boy to go missing too? Something was afoot, and he needed to get to the bottom of it.

He scrubbed a hand along his bristly jaw as he nodded at Sawyer. "I want you to update Rignor with this new development and have him take your place at the warehouse docks. Someone must remain there at all times, alert to any happenings. Meanwhile, you and I shall be riding to the tavern. We will find Lewiston and secure an answer." To his groomsman, he called out, "Parker! Saddle two fresh horses. Sawyer and I shall be riding out shortly."

"Right away, my lord." Parker disappeared into the stables.

Donnelly charged across the front lawn, Woodman awaiting him at the front door, his butler having not missed his conversation or the directives he'd issued to Sawyer. Good. He wouldn't need to repeat himself.

Inside, he strode then stormed up the stairs and entered his study, Woodman directly behind him. He removed his greatcoat and hat and tossed them to his man as he sat at his desk. "How is Lady Maria?" he asked, needing to check on his sister's welfare.

"Still abed, my lord. There have been no disturbances during the night."

"Ensure that remains the case. For now, pack me a

satchel with clothing, along with items which will allow me to blend in with the locals at the Boar Head Tavern. I'll also take a tray in my chamber once I'm done here. I have letters to write, which can't wait."

Keeping his word to Sophia, he penned a quick note to let her know of his return and subsequent change of plans for the day. Then once done, he penned a second letter to her brother. He had to ensure Winterly knew of his feelings for Sophia, that he would claim her for himself, as soon as he possibly could.

Lord Winterly,

We have known each other for some time and I consider you a friend and firm confidant. As such, you should know that I will always be completely loyal in my affections toward your sister. Lady Sophia is a ray of sunshine which I desperately need in my life.

I have barely survived these past few months being parted from her, so once my investigations into my father and brother's deaths are complete and justice is served, I shall be paying a call on you for your sister's hand in marriage.

Yours in trust,
Donnelly.

He folded both letters separately, sealed each with his ring, blew on the hot wax and scrawled Sophia's name on her missive and Winterly's on the other. He handed both letters to Woodman who had returned and quietly remained at attention on the other side of his desk. "Have a footman deliver these letters to Lady Sophia Trentbury and the Earl of Winterly at Winterly's townhouse, not straight away, but in a few hours when their household would have awakened."

"I shall instruct the footman, my lord. Your tray also awaits you in your chamber, and your satchel has been given to Parker to add to your saddlebags. I have secured clothing which will allow you to blend in with ease along the eastern docks, and which is now laid out on your bed."

"Good. See to those letters then aid me in my chamber."

Woodman clipped his polished heels together and disappeared with the letters in hand.

Donnelly strode down the hallway and entered his room, logs crackling in his fireplace and his shaving utensils laid out. Shaving each morning always allowed him a few minutes to sit and reflect before the new day began.

"Take a seat, my lord." Woodman closed the door behind him, crossed to the side table and poured a finger of liquid from the decanter into a crystal glass, then handed it to him.

"Thank you." He eased into the blue patterned wingchair. Woodman had served his father before him, was loyal, dedicated, and had an uncanny ability to know exactly what he needed before he even did. He tipped the brandy back. "Walter, have you ever loved a woman?"

"Yes, although a long time ago." His man dipped the shaving brush into the basin of water and foamed the bar of soap. "Unfortunately, she passed away before we had the chance to wed."

"What was her name? If you don't mind me asking?"

"Miss Meghan Miller." With a heartfelt smile, Woodman laid a cloth at his neck then dabbed the foam across his jaw and chin. "I think about her often, how different my life would have been if we'd had the chance to speak vows as we'd intended on doing. My Meghan had the sweetest smile and the most loyal disposition. I loved her from the moment we first met." Woodman gently scraped his blade from his ear to his chin. "Although she could also be stubborn, particularly when her mind was set, but her stubbornness only made me love and cherish her more."

"She sounds like someone else I know."

"If we are speaking of Lady Sophia, then yes. She shows the same stubborn streak as my Meghan did." Another draw of the blade, along his chin and down his neck.

"You said she passed away. How did that happen?"

"While walking to the village, she was accosted by a thief and took a brutal blow to her head. She managed to stumble home and give her father a description of the assailant, although the next morning she wouldn't awaken from her night's rest. She remained unconscious for the next three days before finally breathing her last." Woodman's voice filled with sadness, his eyes watering. "The pain I experienced that day will always remain strong. We all stood at her bedside, her parents, brothers and sisters, and myself. That day I vowed to always honor Meghan's memory."

"You have done so by sharing your story with me. I'm so sorry you lost her."

"We have all suffered loss, although the only way to

move forward is to remember those who have passed on, and not by their death, but by how they lived their lives." Woodman swiped under his nose then dabbed the remaining suds with a cloth and washed the utensils in the basin. "You honor your father and brother's memory by seeking to uncover their killer. They would be proud of you for doing so."

"I shall see justice served, however I can." Which meant readying himself to ride out for the eastern docks and discover what had happened to Captain Lewiston. He removed his boots, shucked his clothes then pulled on the faded gray trousers and shirt laid on his bed. The linen was rough and abrasive against his skin, the neckcloth which might have been white years ago, was now a mottled yellow. He slipped his arms inside the gray jacket, one completely out of fashion then tugged on a pair of worn riding boots that must belong to one of his groomsmen. He'd have to thank the men who'd offered him their clothing when he returned.

Dressed, he arched a brow at Woodman as his man walked in a slow circle around him. "Will I pass as a dockworker?"

"You shall, my lord, provided you mind how you speak."

"A good point. I'll take care." He opened the top drawer of his oak dresser, removed his pistol and pocketed it.

A nod of approval from his man who gestured to his untouched breakfast tray.

"I wish I had an appetite." Still, he needed the strength and nourishment the food would provide, so he wolfed down the bacon and eggs then taking the stairs two at a time, bounded through the foyer, his current mission set.

He had to find Captain Lewiston and the cabin boy, and he needed to find them without losing his own life. He'd never leave Sophia or his sister behind, not as his father and brother had left them.

Chapter 10

Sophia sat downstairs in Winterly's study, directly behind his chunky oak desk, her brother having had an appointment in town and knowing he wouldn't have minded if she'd borrowed some desk space, she'd commandeered his study and had now written a long and lovely letter to Harry. Everyone else in the house had already written their own letters earlier this morning, so she added hers to the pile of their correspondence and slipped each of the letters inside a canvas carry case for delivery.

"My lady, a letter has arrived for you, and one for his lordship too." Jeeves, his dark mustache curled at the corners and his jacket buttoned, extended a silver tray to her with two letters upon it, her name scrawled across one and her brother's name across the other.

"Thank you." She accepted the letters, placed Winterly's on his desk where he wouldn't miss it, and passed Jeeves the carry case. "Please have these letters delivered to Captain Poole at the Horse Guards in Whitehall, with a request to hand them to Major Harry Trentbury."

"I'll have one of the footmen deliver it immediately."
A dip of the butler's head and he strode from the room.

Settling back in her brother's plush upholstered chair, the fire crackling in the hearth and spreading its warmth over her, she trailed her finger over her name written across her letter. A surge of butterflies took flight in her belly at seeing James's precise hand. She'd never mistake it, not after reading his letter this morning in her chamber. She pressed the thick parchment to her heart and closed her eyes. This letter she'd get to keep, which brought her thoughts veering back to last night.

Oh my, so magical. She couldn't wait to see him again, and even though he'd told her she wasn't permitted to allow him entrance into her room, she'd never be able to turn him away should he tap at her window as he'd done last night.

Smiling, she broke the seal and unfolded the paper.

My sweet Sophia,

I wish this letter was of a brighter subject, but I've returned home this morning to an urgent matter which has arisen, and which I must see to immediately. The Fortune Maria has arrived in port and Captain Lewiston has gone missing, a cabin boy as well. I shall be riding to the Boar Head Tavern near the eastern docks to speak to the captain's brother, Geoffrey Lewiston, who owns the establishment. Hopefully, I can uncover what's happened and return with the captain and lad henceforth. Until my return, please know that I hold you close to my heart.

Yours always,
James.

Her heart clenched in on itself.

Goodness, this wasn't good news at all.

Surely the captain wouldn't have left his post without good reason?

Rising, she tucked James's letter in the pocket of her dark blue skirts and paced her brother's study. Beyond the forest-green drapes framing the wide window, murky gray clouds smeared the afternoon skies from horizon to horizon. Drizzle still fell, as it had earlier this morning when she'd kissed James farewell at the side door.

Fear and worry for him swarmed her middle.

She halted in front of her brother's shelves housing all manner of reading material, including fine works written by the masters. Slotted on the top shelf were French, Spanish, and Italian tomes, along with a wide selection of poetry. The middle shelf held her brother's favorite journals by the most prominent inventors of their time. She ran her finger along the spines of a few, then gasped as she tapped the final book along the shelf. A Minerva Press novel—*Peculiar Warnings*. She'd never noticed this book within their collection before, although Mama often swapped out reading material. One of Mama's dear friends enjoyed reading the Minerva novels for their mystery and intrigue.

She tipped the book out of its slot and opened it.

Chapter One

Soon after the clay-cold body of Count Clement had been discovered in the library by his eldest son, Count Colbert, the deeply distressed son thrust tomes from the library shelves and grasped the one he sought which opened the secret cabinet his late father had used to deposit his papers of great consequence. The son scoured the hidden cabinet, his examination in earnest, and thankfully uncovered what he most ardently required. His younger brother would be overwhelmed with inexpressible grief when he learnt of their father's demise, to the same devastating extent which now swallowed him whole, but these papers were of extreme importance, and he must ensure his brother received them. They proved, beyond a doubt, that their father's death hadn't come by natural means. No, and should he perish soon after his father, then his younger brother would know foul play was most assuredly afoot.

Hands shaking, she sank into one of the two forest-green corner padded chairs sitting either side of the lit fireplace. Had James's father chosen this particular novel of horror to hide his drawing within for a reason? The first page certainly held shocking similarities to what had unfolded at Donnelly House. A father's death, not by natural means. Two sons, both who would grieve greatly. Hidden papers of great consequence. Foul play afoot.

When she'd visited the old earl only the day before his death, he'd been seated before the latticed library window as he'd held a burgundy leather-bound ledger in hand. They'd sat together and he'd spoken of the Fortune Maria having sailed into port earlier than expected, that Captain Lewiston had brought in additional cargo from a sunken vessel, including a treasure chest. They'd spoken of his favorite books and philosophical essays, as well as Marco Polo's book. He'd stood and crossed to the shelf of

Minerva novels and tapped the spine of one slightly out of—oh my. Had that been a sign? That's when Mr. Taylor had arrived to speak to him about the burgundy ledger he'd been perusing upon her arrival, and since she hadn't wished to hold up his meeting with his man of affairs, she'd excused herself and returned to the drawing room where she'd joined Maria.

Her chest heaved, her heart beating sluggish and slow. She'd told James about speaking to his father in his library, but not of all the finer details surrounding that visit, that his father had tapped the Minerva novel and spoken to Mr. Taylor who'd arrived.

The foreseer had told Captain Bourbon she would need his assistance in a matter of the heart, that she would not be aware of all she knew, and that Bourbon would need to keep her close until all was unraveled. Throughout the days ahead, the captain was supposed to be her minder and to keep her safe. Of course James didn't wish for her aid, but only because he worried about dragging her into his investigations, but he had no choice in that regard. She would do whatever was needed to help him.

She also trusted Captain Anteros Bourbon, and she needed to speak to him about what she'd remembered. She settled once more at her brother's desk and penned a precise note to Bourbon, informing him about Captain Lewiston going missing and James's decision to ride to the eastern docks, to the Boar Head Tavern belonging to Geoffrey Lewiston. She gave him the address for the Frederick's masked charity ball and asked him to meet her there, as soon as he could.

Once done, she called out to Jeeves and handed him

her sealed letter. She asked him to have it delivered to The Cobra, Bourbon's gaming hell near the docks, where he'd told her she could reach him. Once Jeeves had left, she stoppered the ink bottle and set the quill to one side, then with jittery fingers, paced the room. Would she be able to inform Anteros of what she'd remembered in time? So he might track down James and warn him?

"Sophia, there you are." Olivia swished into the room, her gown for tonight's masked charity ball a confection of peach colored silk and cream lace, her gown exposing her curves with its cinched bodice and flaring skirts. "Why are you still closeted in Winterly's study when you should be dressing for the ball?"

"Time has run away on me today. You look absolutely breathtaking."

"Thank you, but I'm at an impasse with which mask to wear. Which one do you like best?" Olivia held two masks in her hands and lifted the first to her eyes then the second. "The silk and lace mask?" she asked. "Or the one with feathers?"

"Feathers, although with your golden locks you'll still be unmistakable to those who know you, even with the mask donned. Don't move." She stepped past her sister, peeked out the door and once assured no one stood within the foyer, faced her sister once more. "I have something of great importance to tell you."

"Oh my, this sounds intriguing." Olivia stepped closer. "Do tell."

"Tonight, I've organized a meeting with Captain Anteros Bourbon at the ball."

"You have?" Her eyes went wide. "But you're smitten

with Donnelly and there isn't a chance your feelings for him have changed. Why would you wish to meet with Captain Bourbon?"

"Our meeting is in regard to Donnelly and his current investigations regarding his father and brother. Donnelly has been called to the eastern docks on an urgent matter and I'm not sure how long he'll be away. I've also just come into possession of some crucial information which I must alert Donnelly to. Since I can't, speaking to Bourbon is my only alternative. He'll know how to reach Donnelly quickly."

"Then you've made the right decision to meet with Bourbon." Olivia hugged her tight. "When Bourbon joined us for luncheon at the museum, he seemed open as he spoke of his travels across the Atlantic and yet also elusive at the same time. He is rather intriguing, don't you think?"

"What if I told you that one day you will offer him an olive branch?"

"The symbol of peace?" A frown marred her sister's forehead. "Whatever for?"

"A foreseer told him that one day you'd be his saving grace, an angel sent to him at a time when he would need one the most."

"I beg your pardon?" More confusion. "Do foreseers even exist?"

"I haven't personally met one, but I do believe he has. The seer sent him to me, knowing I'd need his aid."

"Well, that is the truth." A conceding nod. "You've most certainly needed aid with Donnelly."

"Thank you for understanding my plight."

"You would do anything for Donnelly, as I would do

anything for you." Olivia kissed her cheek. "Since you must speak with Bourbon tonight, you must ready yourself for the ball so we can be away immediately. Upstairs with you now."

"Yes, I must hurry." She swept upstairs with Donnelly's letter in her pocket.

In her chamber, she bathed quickly, washing her hair then sitting before the fire to dry her locks. Her maid brushed her hair until the strands curled into a glittering fall down her back.

Abby aided her in dressing and once clothed, she stood before her tall-standing oval mirror and swished from side to side in her gown. Fine golden lace overlaid the skin-colored silk lining, this creation designed to deceive the eye of the beholder, to make them believe at first glance she wore nothing underneath the lace. Surely, it was the most daring gown she'd ever worn, yet her dressmaker had insisted this style would soon be all the rage and with the event being a masked ball, she could hold onto her anonymity for the entire night if she so wished.

She twirled in a full circle, her heart almost alighting from her chest, the lace rippling in a watery golden fall. At the time she'd taken receipt of this gown, Donnelly had yet to join the hussars and her hope had been for him to see her in it. He never would, but she could don it for him in private at the first opportunity. That she'd most certainly do.

"Oh, my lady." Abby fluttered her hands over her mouth. "You look like a princess."

"That is so sweet of you to say." She sat before her mirrored dresser and nodded at Abby to arrange her hair.

Her maid worked her golden locks in a Grecian hairstyle with curls atop her head which exposed the length of her nape, the odd lock dangling free.

Jewelry. She opened the lid of her carved box and selected her favorite gold and pearl earrings and handed them to Abby. Her maid slotted them into her ears and with the matching necklace hooked around her neck, added the last defining piece of her ensemble—the mask.

Abby secured the mask of golden plumes and lace at the back of her head with a silk ribbon, and once she had, she thanked her maid and accepted the matching golden gloves and tugged them on. At the door, Abby draped her white fur cloak over her shoulders and she swept downstairs.

In the foyer, Olivia shrieked when she descended, her sister's smile wide beneath her own mask.

Mama gasped from beside Olivia. "Oh, my dear." Mama rushed forward and clasped her hands. "You look exquisite."

"So do you, Mama." She kissed each of Mama's cheeks, her indigo-colored gown pleated with lace over satin, her mask a glittery tinge of the same deep indigo shade. "You don't think this gown is too daring?"

"It is daring, but superbly so. Madam Gonnier has outdone herself with this creation. Both my daughters shall be the talk of the ball."

"Are you feeling well now?" she asked Mama, who certainly appeared fully recovered.

"Absolutely." A flutter of Mama's fan. "I've been anticipating this masked ball for many months and I'd never allow any illness to force me to miss it."

"Good evening, ladies," Winterly called from the top of the stairs. He descended in fine cream silk pantaloons and a red-tailed coat with blue piping, his cream shirt adorned with ruffles and a red sash overtop. A red silk mask covered his eyes, his hand firm around the curved head of his cane as he halted in front of them. Pressing a kiss to the top of each of their heads, he murmured his approval. "Well, when I walk in with you three beauties on my arms, I shall be the toast of the town, envied across all of England. Are we all ready to depart?"

"We are," Mama answered with a grin. "You escort your sisters while I lead the way." Mama swished out the door which Jeeves opened for them.

"Escort, I shall." Winterly extended an arm to her and Olivia and steered them both outside and down the driveway in Mama's eager wake. He aided all three of them into their awaiting coach and stepped inside. Sophia sat on the rear burgundy padded seat next to Olivia, Mama and Winterly across from her and with a rap of her brother's cane on the ceiling, Winterly called out to their driver, "To Frederick House."

The slap of the reins resounded, and the horses soon settled into a smooth gait. They traversed the streets toward the most exclusive residential area in London, the skies darkening and the moon rising high. Leaning forward, Sophia gasped at the sight of carriages lining both sides of the street. Their coach moved slowly forward in short spurts as they awaited their turn to draw up to the entrance. Such a magnificent, palatial house.

It stood three stories high with its front rooms ablaze with candlelight.

Finally they came to a complete stop and an elegant, liveried footman opened the door.

Winterly handed them down and the excited buzz of the guests swept over them as they wandered along the front walk.

Sophia entered the grand foyer, her eyes going wide at the mass of attendees. There had to be at least seven hundred people present in this ballroom alone, not to mention how many more would be circulating about the other rooms of the house. With Olivia at her side and Winterly and Mama directly behind her, she made her way past a uniformed servant, who took their cloaks and secured a dance card to her wrist with a white ribbon, then did so for Olivia as well.

A few steps farther, she and her sister accepted a fluted glass of champagne from a passing waiter and clinked their glasses together.

Mr. Tidmore, their brother's business partner in his maritime trade ventures, joined them with his fluted glass in hand, a deep blue tailcoat donned over a white shirt and red breeches, his mask adorned with the same red, white, and blue colors. "Ladies," he said with an extravagant bow. "You all look radiant this evening. Your brother is certainly a fortunate man to be escorting such beauties."

"Yes, fortunate indeed." Winterly clapped Tidmore on the back and the two men launched into a lively discussion about their merchant ship which had just arrived into port earlier that day.

"Oh, there's Lady Foxeworth," Mama gushed. "She mentioned her mask would be a soft lavender, the same as her evening gown. I must speak to her about the gathering she'll be holding later this week at her home. Excuse me, my dears, I won't be long." Mama bustled away.

Perfect. With her brother and mother's attention diverted elsewhere, she could search for Anteros, with Olivia's aid. She cooled herself with a flick of her golden-feathered fan, the chatter of the crowd drifting over her. Leaning into Olivia, she whispered in her ear, "Help me look out for Captain Bourbon. The sooner I speak to him, the better."

"He might be hard to spot in this crowd, although with his dark hair and towering height, perhaps not. He must be a good hand over six feet." Olivia tapped one slippered toe to the lively tune as she searched through the eye slits of her mask for Bourbon, her gaze moving over the dancing couples under the crystal chandeliers which shimmered with light.

"Since he's a spymaster, I have the feeling we shall only see him when he wishes to be seen." Sophia searched each corner and darkened nook. Nothing so far. Toward the doors leading out onto the balcony, layers of cream silk draped the doorways and swooped across the tops of the windows, the elaborate decorations Grecian in style. Marble statues, busts, and high swaying palms graced various spots where people grouped together. Large numbers circled the refreshment table, and a group of masked gentlemen in dark tailcoats and glasses in hand, wandered out of the room down a wide passageway, likely to enjoy some respite offered in the games' rooms.

A hush settled over the room and Olivia clutched a hand to her chest. "Look, Sophia, there's Prince George."

Prinny strode in wearing hose and knee-length gold

silk pantaloons, a gold brocade waistcoat with a gold-lace ruffled cravat at his neck and a red and gold brocade overcoat open, his cuffs and high collar embroidered with gold. White gloves and pointed black shoes holding wide buckles completed his elegant look, his hair powdered white and fluffed high at the top and his mask covering his eyes. Inarguably, he was a patron of style and taste, although his dissolute way of life dimmed his appeal dramatically. He'd had countless affairs since his marriage to Princess Caroline, bedding actresses, divorced wives, songwriters, as well as the current wives of older gentlemen of the peerage. His entourage followed him, of courtiers and a lady considered his current mistress, the woman bedecked in jewels and wearing an elaborate gown and mask.

As protocol demanded, Sophia swept into a deep curtsy as the prince passed by, her knees bent and head slightly bowed, her skirts held outward. Thankfully, he moved on quickly and eased into a regal chair placed at the head of the ballroom where waiters and servants scurried to bring him wine and food overflowing from silver platters.

"*Disgustoso.*" A grunt from behind them. "The prince strolls in here with a sinful amount of pomp and ceremony, all while displaying his mistress to one and all."

"I couldn't agree more." Sophia turned and curtsied to Captain Bourbon, the spymaster attired head to toe in black with no other adornment save for the large diamond which twinkled from his right ear. With his black satin mask hiding his expression, the captain oozed mystery with his jet-black hair slicked back and his blue eyes shining as deep and as bottomless as rich sapphires. He appeared dark and dangerous, a man one didn't trifle with unless they enjoyed said danger, and going by the interested look in her sister's eyes, Olivia was in fact completely intrigued by that danger.

Sophia tapped her closed fan against the captain's jacketed arm. "Kind sir, you must have received my letter without any issue."

"I did, then secured an invitation to this elaborate ball and stepped into my carriage immediately." He caught her gloved hand and kissed her knuckles before lifting Olivia's hand and kissing her sister's fingertips. With a soft murmur, he said, "*Un bellissimo angelo.* You look radiant tonight."

"Captain." A soft sigh escaped Olivia's lips then she promptly tugged her hand back. "My papa once warned me that when a man lavishes such words of praise on a lady, that she should take immense care around him. You seem to be a dangerous puzzle I can't quite work out."

"Your papa was clearly a wise man." His lips tugged up into a sinful grin. "Might I add my own words of warning to his?"

"Go right ahead." A challenging tilt to Olivia's head.

"When a man collects enemies at every turn, just as I have a habit of unfortunately doing, you should steer clear of that man. Immense care must be taken."

"I, ah—" Olivia glanced at her, then back at Bourbon. "Your warning has been duly noted."

"Good evening, Lady Olivia." A masked gentleman whisked in and picked up her sister's dance card. He signed his name alongside the next two dances. This had to be Baron Herbarth. Only he ever attempted to commandeer

Olivia's card at every ball they attended. The baron was simply smitten with her sister.

"Lord Herbarth, how did you know it was me?" Olivia voice was pitched a little too high. "Goodness, reserving two dances with a lady on one night will cause a stir and my mama will end up having words with me. I'm certain we've spoken of this before."

"Yes, we have, but hopefully your mama will speak only wonderful words." The baron chuckled as he eyed Olivia. "Surely, you can't fault me for wishing to dance with such a delightful companion. I'm certain you'll be inundated with gentlemen and I didn't wish to miss out."

A low growl emanated from Bourbon, his sapphire eyes hardening to a deeply black hue.

"You collect enemies, remember?" Olivia pressed a hand to Bourbon's arm then batted her lashes at Herbarth. "Sir, I believe you are right, and I shall concede to two dances."

"Wonderful. I always enjoy your delightful conversation and clever wit when we dance." Herbarth placed one hand behind his back and bowed as he offered Olivia his arm. "My lady, will you join me in dancing the next set together?"

"I'd be delighted." Olivia accepted the baron's arm and moved away into the swirling mass of dancers.

"Your sister tugs on the tail of *the cobra* with her actions." Bourbon extended his hand to Sophia, his head dipped and gaze steadfast on hers. "Might I request this dance, my lady?"

"Are you certain the foreseer said that Olivia would one day be your saving grace?" She placed her fingers in his and walked with him onto the dancefloor.

"Yes, an angel sent to me at a time when I would need one the most, only I've no desire to get too close to your sister." He swept her in amongst the couples, directly into the same set which Olivia and the baron had joined.

"It doesn't appear that's the case. You gravitate toward her with ease." The chords of a new dance began. She pointed her right toe and sank elegantly down on her left leg into a curtsy.

"Your sister could be my very downfall," Bourbon murmured as he glanced at Olivia, who also snuck a glance at him under her lashes.

"That sounds ominous. Why do you say such a thing?"

"I adore the wide-open seas and find I'm often gone from England for months at a time. Meanwhile, your sister needs to remain here. I can't have her forcing me to remain here with her." He bowed deeply with a royal swish of one hand behind his back. "Have I mentioned I have a sister of my own, one who enjoys finding trouble? I'm constantly scouring the seas for her and dragging her back to safety."

"Sisters can be troublesome, and you don't yet know Olivia all that well. She actually adores traveling, not that she's ever traveled any farther than our fair land." As slow and graceful as she could, she circled to Anteros's right, their fingers touching ever so softly, their gazes on each other. "Pray tell, what is your sister's name?"

"Adrestia." He smiled softly as he moved about her, his love for his sister clear to see in his eyes. "She is a rascal, a *splendido* rascal."

"She holds a Greek name the same as you do."

"Yes, one given to the children born of Ares and

Aphrodite. My mother's fascination with all things Roman or Greek always knew no bounds. During my childhood, she named each of our pets after the Greek gods."

"Oh, how interesting. I would enjoy meeting your mother and your sister. We must arrange such a visit."

"My mother isn't available for visits, but my sister will be, when I next find her." A chuckle. "She is currently sailing the seas."

"She sounds delightful." She stepped back and moved toward Olivia then circled her sister.

"What on earth are you two whispering about?" Olivia's eyes blazed with curiosity behind her mask.

"You, my dear sister, and Anteros's mother and sister." She bit her lip in an attempt to stifle her giggle, which she barely managed to do. "I have asked that we arrange a visit so we might meet them. He said his mother isn't available, but his sister will be, once he finds her. She is currently sailing the seas."

"You truly asked if we might meet his family?" Shock widened her sister's eyes, then they narrowed with annoyance. "Are you matchmaking, dear sister?"

"Possibly, or perhaps the fates have already spoken."

"Pardon?" Olivia gritted her teeth as the dance forced her to move away. Her sister circled Bourbon and they spoke quietly to each other, whispered words Sophia missed, but by the deep chuckle Anteros released as he stepped back from Olivia, clearly their discussion had amused him.

Anteros moved around her next. "Olivia's *passione* for life is invigorating."

"My sister embraces every challenge that comes her

way, and I believe you present a challenge to her." The dance separated them again, and Sophia moved around Herbarth. She offered the baron a smile, then moved in division, aligning with the third lady in their set, then back to Anteros again.

He swept a hand around her back and guided her in a circle. "In your letter, you updated me on Donnelly's movements, of the Fortune Maria arriving in port without Captain Lewiston, that Donnelly has ridden to the Boar Head Tavern near the eastern docks to speak to the captain's brother, Geoffrey Lewiston."

"Indeed, and also while in my brother's study this afternoon I uncovered something of great import. Might we speak somewhere about it, in private of course, where we won't be overheard?"

"Most certainly." He glanced at a masked man standing in the shadows next to the passageway and flicked a finger. The man gave the captain a firm nod.

"Who is that?" she asked as Anteros guided her out of the ballroom under a wide arch.

"Giovani, a man I trust with my life." He led her along a winding passageway, the lit candles in each wall sconce flickering eerily. At the end of the walkway, Anteros opened a door with stairs leading downward into the gloomy depths of the cellars.

Cobwebs hung from the corners, the walls gritty and pitted, the overpowering scent of dampness swirling from somewhere within the murky depths far below.

"This is an interesting place for a private meeting." She shuddered and rubbed her bare arms.

Chapter 11

Donnelly tugged the sides of his hooded cloak closer to ward off the chill, the fog-shrouded night in the east end of London dense and dark. Slouching a little and keeping his chin down, he pushed open the door of the Boar Head Tavern and stepped inside.

The crowded room was filled with men swigging drinks and enjoying a meal, while a fire roared in the hearth along the far wall. Sawyer sat hunched in one darkened corner, his head hidden within the folds of his hood, the acrid scent of sweat, spilled ale and fried food clogging the air. He'd sent Sawyer in ahead of him to do reconnaissance since he didn't wish for any of the patrons to wonder if they were together, not when they had the captain to locate and information to uncover. Sliding into the closest booth where he'd be afforded a good view of the room, he lifted a hand to the barmaid as she circled the tables.

She flounced up to him, her bountiful breasts almost spilling from the low neckline of her blue kirtle. "Ye hailed me, my lovely?"

"Bring me some ale." He kept his voice low, inflicting

an edge to match the speech of those in this darker part of London.

"Do ye wish for a meal too?" Raising one appreciative eyebrow, she leaned in even farther and he couldn't miss the peek of pink nipple she exposed. "The bread is fresh from the ovens and the stew thick and chunky."

"Just the ale."

"Come now." She tsked under her breath. "A big man like ye must surely have a hearty appetite. I have a room below-stairs if ye wish a tumble."

"My tumbling days are reserved for one woman alone."

"Have a wife do ye? Well, should ye change yer mind"—winking, she swished her bottom in front of his face—"then ye know where to find me."

"I won't be changing my mind, but thank ye all the same." Since she continued to wag her backside at him, he swatted her rear, which thankfully sent her into giggles and off on her way.

"I'm telling ye, he said he'd pay us well for sailing with him. There are riches to be had across the seas." A big-bellied man who'd had a pint too many and slightly slurred his words, waggled one brow at the other men at his table, a silver hoop looped through one of his ears. "Pirating is a merry way to go, lads. Tortuga holds a nest of excitement, with gold flowin'. There's rum and revelry, wenches and plenty o' rutting."

"I've got me a wife and child, Bolider. I can't be leavin' 'em." A lanky young man with a thin face and dark circles under his eyes, shoved one hand through his scruffy hair. "My wife would have me hide if I took off."

"A few months at sea and a bit o' time for squandering our riches. Surely, ye can leave them for a wee bit, Johnny. Ye pockets would be overflowin' with coin." More urging from the man called Bolider.

The barmaid returned and set Donnelly's ale down.

She sashayed away and moved around the men's table, then plopped a platter of greasy sausages in the center, her kirtle flaring wide over her ample hips. All the men shoveled sausages into their mouths, oil dribbling down their chins.

"Ye have fine fare, lass." Bolider smirked as he grabbed the wench's breasts and squeezed them. "I wouldn't mind takin' a bite out o' ye."

"I won't be sharing any of my fine fare with ye again, not when ye never give me a coin for my troubles." She seized Bolider's tankard and downed a mouthful of his ale. Giving him a feisty look, she muttered in his ear, "Thirsty I am, but fer a man who can sweep me off my feet."

"Come now, Meg. Captain Lewiston gave ye enough coin for the both of us when he last flipped ye skirts. I had to have a go at ye too, and he didn't mind none. Ye didn't mind it either at the time."

Captain Lewiston. Donnelly's ears perked up and so did Sawyer's, his man straightening where he sat on the other side of the rowdy men.

"I'll join ye at sea, Bolider." A dark bearded man with his grimy shirtsleeves rolled to his elbows lifted his tankard to his lips. "There be no one keepin' me tied to hearth and home."

"Me either," a rough looking red-head said with a leer. "What o' ye, Fraser?"

Another yes came from the man called Fraser, then the one named Johnny slowly nodded with half a sausage still in his mouth. "Damn me, but I'll find a way to tell the missus I'm joinin' ye."

"Good lad, the captain will be pleased." Bolider slapped Johnny on the back. "All of ye need to be at the eastern docks in four hours. Find *The Renegade*. We set sail on the dawn's high tide." Bolider dunked his head into the barmaid's bosom and grunted as he swiped a tongue out.

Meg lifted his head and laughing, shoved a sausage in his mouth. "Eat ye food and cease slobberin' over me."

"I'll give ye coin this time, lass, and I'll sweep ye off yer feet too," he rumbled as he stabbed his teeth into the sausage and broke the crispy skin. He scraped his chair back, tossed the wench over his shoulder and slid one hand under her skirts. A slap of her backside and he marched down the darkened corridor leading off the main room, his footsteps echoing and the barmaid's giggles following.

Four hours. That's all the blasted time he and Sawyer had to halt Lewiston from setting sail.

"Oi, ye got a problem?" A hand slammed down on his shoulder.

Donnelly swiveled around, the bloke before him both familiar yet also not.

"What? Cat got ye tongue?" The man jutted out his whiskered chin, a scar slashing his face either side of a leather eye patch strung over his right eye. "I haven't seen ye in my tavern afore."

"Are ye the owner of this fine establishment?" he asked.

"I just said so."

Then he must be Captain Lewiston's brother, Geoffrey Lewiston. That's why he appeared familiar. He had the same high forehead and pointed nose as Captain Lewiston. Taking care, Donnelly slowly rose to his feet. "The name's Jack. I'm lookin' fer work. Bolider said Captain Lewiston would pay them well." He hoisted one thumb over his shoulder at the table of men. "I've been to Tortuga a time or two and know the waters well."

"Who have ye sailed with?" Geoffrey eyed him up and down.

"The Hawk." He named the wild and rugged pirate who terrorized the warmer seas around the Americas. "We parted ways."

"Interesting." Geoffrey puffed out his chest, the glitter of jade pinned within the man's billowy white shirt glinting at him. Exquisitely carved and in the shape of a skull-and-bones, the jade pin matched the one recorded in his father's papers from within the treasure chest.

He'd hit a windfall tonight. About damn time.

"'Tis fine ale ye serve." Donnelly swept up his tankard and saluted the man.

"Hawk, ye say? Well, now I understand why ye seemed mighty interested in their conversation. If ye survived Hawk then ye'll survive my brother and I. Get yerself down to the docks before the high tide. The Renegade sets sail from these shores soon, and we intend on terrorizing the same seas as The Hawk does. We're after loot, and plenty of it."

"Geoffrey!" A plump man at the bar wiping a jug with a cloth gestured toward the front door. A new arrival, the gentleman holding his chin high, his cravat impeccably tied and his finely woven jacket and tan breeches holding not a wrinkle.

"Blackburne," Geoffrey called as he strode across to the man. "Have ye come to make an offer on my tavern? I wish to leave it in worthy hands."

Donnelly flicked up his collar and turned away so Blackburne wouldn't notice him, not that he'd met the man before, but he had seen him on occasion when he'd accompanied Prince George to a ball. Blackburne, a young and brash solicitor, advised England's future king on business issues and was known to have become one of Prinny's favorites amongst the men he kept as counsel. He also happened to be the man Bourbon had snuck the jade mask from. He'd more than hit a windfall tonight. He'd uncovered the jackpot.

"We close the deal right now." Blackburne pumped Geoffrey's hand. "I need a business such as yours in this east end of town to expand my trade."

"Ye will be well satisfied with this tavern. Come to my office." Geoffrey led the solicitor down the passageway.

Gritting his teeth, Donnelly strode out the front door and into the foggy drizzle. Underneath a flickering lamp, he marched then continued on down the sidewalk. Shadows lurked between the buildings and down the alleyways. He took a hard right and halted at the end of the street to await Sawyer.

His man appeared out of the swirling mist, his coat cloaking him.

Pacing back and forth under the lamp, he muttered to his man, "Captain Lewiston isn't leaving port, or his nefarious brother."

"They're both as thick as thieves, my lord. Did you see the jade pin on Geoffrey? Pompous ass," Sawyer muttered as he kept his hooded gaze watchful on the street either side of them.

"I did, and we'll deal with Geoffrey later." He'd never considered Captain Lewiston as the thief, not when he'd been so loyal to his father over the years. Clearly though, greed changed a man. Which left a glaring question.

Lewiston had sailed from port before his father had perished, so even though he'd stolen the chest, he couldn't be the killer. He clenched his fists, his knuckles going white. "We'll bring Lewiston in, with our bare hands if need be, his brother too."

"I'll be right by your side." Sawyer punched one fisted hand into the palm of his other. "I do enjoy a good brawl."

"Then to docks we go. We've a ship to find, and the elusive Captain Lewiston to apprehend."

Chapter 12

Alone with Anteros and his man in the gloomy darkness of the stairwell leading downward into the shadowed depths of the cellars, the meager light from a lamp all that shimmered, Sophia shivered from the cold chill sweeping up from below, the dampness of the gritty walls clogging her nose and mouth.

"Ensure all remains secure," Anteros instructed Giovani and after his man disappeared downstairs to check the cellars, the captain swung his superfine black jacket off and eased it around her shoulders. Once he'd encased her within its warmth, he said, "You told me you've uncovered something of great import in your brother's study. There is no one who will interrupt us here. Speak freely, Sophia."

"The book that contained the drawing of the jade mask was titled *Peculiar Warnings*, and I uncovered the same novel on the bookshelves in my brother's study. After reading the first few lines I was taken aback by the rather ominous similarities between what was written and what had happened to Donnelly's father."

"What were those similarities?" Interest flared in his

eyes.

"The novel spoke of the death of Count Clement, his clay-cold body being discovered in his library by his eldest son. The son, quite distressed at seeing his father on the floor, located a particular tome on one of the bookshelves, thrust it free and uncovered a secret cabinet. Within the cabinet, he removed his late father's papers, those of great consequence."

"There are huge similarities. Continue, please." He gripped her arms. "Leave nothing out."

"The passage stirred my memories. Only a day before the old earl's death, I visited him in his library. He'd been sitting in front of the latticed windows as he'd held a burgundy leather-bound ledger in hand and when I joined him, he set that ledger aside. We chatted, and he showed me some of his favorite books and philosophical essays on his shelves. He stood right next to a series of Minerva novels and tapped the spine of one slightly out of position. It seemed a rather purposeful tap, and that was the exact tome which held the drawing. I can't help but wonder if the old earl was trying to convey some kind of secret message to me. He would have read that book, as he'd read each one in his library."

"Yes, his tapping of the book could easily have been a subtle warning. What happened next?"

"Mr. Taylor arrived to speak to him, and since I hadn't wished to hold up his meeting with his man of affairs, I excused myself and returned to the drawing room where I joined Lady Maria."

"Is Donnelly aware of this?"

"He's aware I spoke to his father the day before his

passing, that we sat together in his library, but I'd completely forgotten about his father tapping the spine of the Minerva novel, or that Taylor arrived to speak to him, so no, he's not aware of everything." She searched Anteros's gaze. "Now Captain Lewiston is missing and Donnelly has gone to Geoffrey Lewiston's tavern to track him down. What are your thoughts? Are we getting closer to uncovering the killer?"

"It isn't possible for Captain Lewiston to have killed Donnelly's father and brother, not when he set sail on the Fortune Maria before the murders took place, but with his disappearance I'd surmise he's our thief, which means the thief and killer aren't one and the same as I'd first suspected. As Donnelly suspects too."

"Do you have any inkling who the murderer is?"

"Not as yet, but I won't halt my investigations until I uncover the killer's identity." He gestured down the stairs into the darkened depths. "A tunnel leads from this cellar below into the rear gardens. My coach awaits me in the rear alleyway."

"You've come prepared for a swift departure?"

"Yes, I've always found it rather advantageous to have a secondary exit point, even from a lavish ball. I'm also leaving now, and considering the seer's grave warning, I must take you with me until all is uncovered."

"Is that the grave warning you didn't yet wish to tell me?"

"Yes, but the time has now come to speak of it. Shira told me that danger awaits on the high tide, that only the lady who wears glittering gold can keep death from coming for the one her heart desires." He motioned to her gown.

"That is you, Sophia. Are you prepared to leave?"

"Of course." She had no intention of allowing James to fall into danger, not now, not ever.

"Captain?" Giovani strode up the stairs, appearing out of the dark as he joined them under the flickering lamplight.

"Does all remain secure?"

"Yes."

"Good. We're leaving, along with Lady Sophia." He plucked the glittering diamond from his ear and passed it to his man. "Find Lady Olivia Trentbury in the ballroom and hand this to her, along with this message. Inform her that her sister is joining me on a mission of great importance to the eastern docks, and that she must hide the truth. Give her my word that I shall keep her sister safe and return her as soon as possible."

"Will do, Captain." Giovani snuck out the door and disappeared back along the passageway toward the ballroom.

Anteros closed the door, lifted the lamp and caught her elbow.

Carefully, he steered her down the stairwell, the lamp's glow guiding their way as he swung it before them. They passed rows of shelved wine then stepped through a doorway and down into the depths of a tunnel.

The cloying odor of dirt and grit strengthened, then a hundred feet on, a wash of fresh night air blew all around and she scrambled out the opening of the tunnel and emerged within the shadows of a clump of thick bushes. A low branch snagged the ribbon of her mask and she pulled it free. Moonlight shimmered over the rear gate of the property and footsteps crunched over fallen leaves.

Giovani appeared and gave Anteros a brief nod that surely meant all had gone well with Olivia, then he unclipped the gate and motioned them through.

"To the Boar Head Tavern, with all haste," Anteros instructed his driver as he aided her directly into the confines of his awaiting coach. With the door closed, he flicked out his tails and sat.

She held onto her seat as the carriage jerked forward, the velvet pads plush and thick, her destination not one she was currently dressed for. "I don't suppose you have a change of clothes on hand?"

"I never leave home without being prepared." From underneath his seat, he pulled a satchel free and opened it between them. He pulled out lad's clothing, a shirt, brown trousers, and a woolen jacket and cap. "These items belong to Wills, a lad in my employ. Wills won't mind if you borrow what you need."

"Thank you."

"Allow me to give you some privacy, or as much as I currently can." He turned and kept his gaze on the scenery out his window, where the moon shimmered down over private driveways leading to stately homes.

"How did you come to employ a lad?" she asked as she removed the jacket he'd slung around her shoulders and not allowing herself a second thought, removed her gown of glittering golden gauze and the pale silk lining. The cooler air washed over her bare skin, but only for a mere moment before she donned the snug trousers and tugged on the coarse shirt.

"Wills wished to escape his former employer, so he

stole a skiff and when a storm passed through he ended up adrift. Pirates plucked him from the sea and sold him to my cousin in Tangier, whom I happened to be visiting at the time. Wills might be savvy with a thick skin, but he also has a heart of gold that will never harden. Since he wouldn't have survived a single month with my cousin, who is unfortunately far too ruthless, I took him with me. Wills is now family to me. Giovani and I watch out for him."

"I see, and is it true that Tangier is a safe haven for spies? Those are the rumors I've heard bandied about here and there." She donned the jacket and stuffed the gray woolen cap over her upswept do, then swapped her slippers for the scuffed leather boots at the bottom of the satchel. "I'm presentable."

"The rumors are very true, which is why I have a home along the Maghreb Coast. A spymaster thrives on being among his fellow spies." The captain faced her, inspected her from head to toe and nodded firmly. "Clearly, I can now no longer sell you for a fortune at the souk in Tangier."

She smiled, his teasing tone breaking the tension. "You honestly would have tried?"

"Yes, even though your sister might never have spoken to me again." Smirking, he plucked weapons out from under the seat, strapped a sword belt on and slotted the curved blade of a saber at his hip. A pistol got pocketed next, then he slid a dagger into his boot.

"You seem to have quite the arsenal on hand. Do you have a spare pistol by chance?" She wouldn't mind some protection herself, even though she'd never touched a weapon in her life.

"Do you know how to use one?" He quirked a brow.

"No, but I'm a quick learner." She folded her gown and tucked it away in the satchel.

"I see, but a smaller, more discreet weapon is what you need." He removed more weaponry from under the bench and opened a slot in the roof before handing them up to Giovani. With the final remaining dagger in hand, he slid the sheathed blade into her boot and tucked her trouser hem over it. "You're now armed, but you must allow Giovani and I to guard and protect you. I give you my word no harm shall come to you."

"Thank you." She patted the dagger, the cold steel reassuring against her skin.

Onward, they rode, while out the window drizzle slicked the cobbled streets and fog rolled in. Brick buildings, blackened with soot, held broken front steps and uneven doors. Shouts and curses mingled with the pounding of their horses' hooves.

When they finally slowed and halted before an inn with a wooden sign swinging above the front door reading *Boar Head Tavern*, she clenched the edge of the window, her fingers frozen.

Two rowdy, drunk men staggered out, one falling onto his face in a mucky puddle. Another man stepped clear of those two, his attire immaculate, a man she'd met before at various balls. She whispered his name, "Blackburne."

"Where?" Anteros slid in front of the window and growled under his breath. "I see him, and his presence here at the Boar Head Tavern is far too coincidental for my liking."

"Isn't he the man you recovered the jade mask from?"

"Yes, of which he bought for a large sum from a contact of his at the eastern docks. Devil take it. He must have purchased it from Geoffrey Lewiston who owns this tavern." He snorted, his gaze narrowing. "I've spoken with Geoffrey Lewiston before, although not recently. Captain Lewiston and his brother are clearly working together."

Blackburne walked past their coach and another man with an eye patch caught up to him. The two men rounded the corner and Anteros scowled.

"Do you know the other man?" she asked him.

"The man with the eye patch is Geoffrey Lewiston." He rapped the ceiling and when Giovani popped his head through the upper slot, he instructed his man, "Tell the driver to discreetly follow both the solicitor and the tavern owner."

They followed the two men to the corner, where Blackburne and Lewiston shook hands and suddenly separated. Blackburne stepped into a carriage and Lewiston strode on toward the docks.

"Who do we follow now?" Giovani asked Bourbon through the slot.

"We know where Blackburne lives and has his offices, so we can catch up with him later. For now, we need to follow Geoffrey Lewiston since he is headed toward the ships moored at berth." Anteros nodded at his man. "That is a jade pin glinting from his shirt."

"I noticed it too," Giovani muttered.

So had Sophia.

She held tight to her seat as they bumped along. Geoffrey strode directly along a walkway toward a three-mast ship at berth, while their coach came to a rocking halt when they could go no farther.

Anteros bounded out, reached back and swung her down beside him.

Giovani, heavily armed, jumped down and joined them.

Anteros tugged the brim of her cap lower over her face and leaned into her ear. "Stay behind me where I know you're safe. That's an order."

"Yes, sir."

Chapter 13

In the dark of the night, Donnelly hauled himself over the side of Lewiston's ship at berth, a formidable three-mast vessel, a floating fortress which couldn't have been purchased without a great deal of coin. Like that contained within the chest. Hell, Captain Lewiston was a despicable thief, one currently standing on the upper deck next to the wheel as he surveyed charts spread across a tabled platform, a lamp burning.

"Brother, I'm here." Geoffrey Lewiston strode up the gangplank and appeared out of the dark, his eye patch in place as he joined Captain Lewiston. Well, it appeared the tavern owner had caught up to him and Sawyer. Good, he could kill two birds with one stone.

Turning back, he offered Sawyer a hand on board. His man snuck over and dropped in beside him. He motioned to Lewiston and his brother at the helm. "I'll take the captain, while you take his brother."

Sawyer nodded.

Keeping low, they crept forward, staying within the shadows along the foredeck where crates were stacked high with provisions yet to be stored below in the hold.

He brushed past one crate and caught the glint of weaponry within. How fortunate. Even though he had a pistol in his pocket, the more weapons he had on hand, the better. He gestured for Sawyer to arm himself, and both of them slid a saber free and slotted daggers in their boots and belts.

"Donnelly?" A rough whisper traveled to him as a man slithered over the side of the ship, a touch of moonlight tracing across his face. Captain Bourbon. A second man snuck over after him, then the two men lifted a lad on board with a cap hiding his face.

He and Sawyer crouched next to Bourbon and he clasped the spymaster's hand. "Good timing. I've not long come from the Boar Head Tavern. Geoffrey Lewiston owns it and has sold it to Blackburne. Both the captain and his brother are here now, due to set sail on the high tide. They're as thick as thieves, Bourbon."

"We followed Geoffrey here from the tavern, right after Blackburne stepped into a coach and left." Bourbon gestured toward his man. "This is Giovani, one of my most trusted men."

"It's good to meet you, Giovani. And the lad?" Donnelly tried to get a better look at the boy, but he kept his head tucked down. "Is it Wills?"

"No, Wills remains at your warehouse, keeping an eye out for me." Bourbon grasped his shoulder. "You need to keep an open mind about what I'm about to say."

"Go ahead."

"I've spoken to you about the foreseer who issued me instructions. She also gave me a grave warning, one I didn't care to ignore, not tonight, not considering all that's occurred."

"I've never met a foreseer, but yours seems to have led you on the right path so far." He had to concede that much.

"Shira is a wise woman." Bourbon released a staggered breath. "With that being the case, I've followed her advice, which means I had to bring Sophia with me tonight. Sophia must also remain until all is uncovered. Your continued safety will be in question otherwise."

His heart dumped to his feet, his ears ringing. Surely, he'd misheard Bourbon. This ship was the last place he wanted Sophia, particularly when a battle was about to unfold. He drew in a deep breath and released it as slowly as he could, then lifted her chin with one finger. Her stubborn blue gaze met his from under the lad's cap. "You shouldn't have come, no matter the grave warning from the seer."

"I had no other choice."

"We need to speak about your inability to follow my orders." Curving his hand around her neck, he dragged her up against him and trying to find some blasted focus with her so close to the battle about to unfold, muttered in her ear, "You're to stay out of sight. Do you understand?"

"I'll remain right here behind these crates." She pressed a hand to his chest. "I'm glad we found you. How are you?"

"Not in the mood for jovial conversation."

"Duly noted." She stared at his mouth, her eyes darkening, then she blinked and lifted her gaze back to his. "We have a thief to capture and contain, along with his nefarious brother. If you get hurt during your coming confrontation with Lewiston, I'll be furious with you."

"Capturing and containing Lewiston and his brother won't be an issue, not when we have them both outnumbered."

"Good. Then this shall be a quick battle, in which we can then return home as soon as you're done." She winked at him, actually winked, then she snuck back behind Bourbon, her next whispered words traveling to him, "It's time to confront these two blackguards and take them down, and preferably before the rest of their crew arrive."

"Yes, time is of the essence," Bourbon added. "Lead the way, Donnelly."

Indeed, he'd lead the way.

Then he'd get Sophia off this ship and back home where she'd be safe.

No more crouching behind crates.

He rose and stormed toward his nemesis. "Lewiston!"

The urge to kill Captain Lewiston thrummed with deadly menace through him.

"Well, well." Lewiston straightened from his charts, his coat flapping about his legs, his sword strapped to his side glinting in the moonlight. "Lord Donnelly, I'd so hoped to be gone from here before you discovered what had become of me."

"You're a thief."

"I beg to differ. I'm the one who retrieved the sunken treasure and had every right to keep a share of it for myself. Unfortunately, your father had a different idea and wouldn't entertain my request for that share. He snubbed his nose at me, stating that as both my employer and the owner of the Fortune Maria, that the fate of the treasure was his to decide. He intended for every blasted piece within the chest to be returned to its rightful owner, although he underestimated me. I snuck into the War Office and filched the chest before handing it over to my brother. While I've been away, Geoffrey has sold enough of it to fund our upcoming expedition. There are riches aplenty across the seas, which will soon be filling our hands."

"I'll never let you or your brother set sail from this wharf." He clenched his fist around his sword hilt.

"Such a shame about your father and brother," Lewiston sneered as he slid his sword from his belt and advanced. "Geoffrey enlightened me about their demise when I arrived in port. I asked him to keep an eye on them and Mr. Taylor."

"Did you or your brother have anything to do with their deaths?" He had to know for certain, if perhaps Geoffrey had done the dastardly deed since Captain Lewiston couldn't have.

"No, of course not, although you should ask Mr. Taylor that question. He most certainly knows a thing or two about their demise." A smirk as he arched a brow. "He's the one who wished them gone, not me. You have my condolences, by the way."

"Why would Taylor wish them gone?"

"Whenever I returned from a voyage with cargo, Taylor handed me enough blunt to keep quiet. He of course, squandered some of the cargo from each shipment and fetched a pretty penny for it. He feared your father's suspicions had been aroused recently, and wisely so. They had been." Swinging his sword in a wide arc, Lewiston gritted his teeth. "Now it's time for your demise."

"It is you who shall perish this night, not me." Donnelly shoved his saber high and met Lewiston's fierce blow.

Behind him, Bourbon, Giovani, and Sawyer strode clear of the crates and formed a half circle at his back.

Over his shoulder, Lewiston bellowed to his brother. "Care to join me?"

"I've been thirsting for a fight." Geoffrey pulled his sword free and bounded down from the helm.

With another shout from Captain Lewiston, two more men swarmed onto the deck from below in the hold.

Sawyer and Giovani swung their blades against the newcomers, while Bourbon squared up to Geoffrey.

Captain Lewiston pushed forward against him, and Donnelly thrust one foot back and tried to hold his position, their blades crossed an inch from his nose.

Steel clanged against steel, an almighty battle unfolding.

Captain Lewiston twirled his blade as he heaved, and they fought hard and fast, the captain's blows well-timed as he worked to take Donnelly down. Blocking each of Lewiston's strikes, he battled hard with every ounce of determination and strength he had, while beside him Sawyer, Bourbon, and Giovani fought against their opponents.

"James, please, you must be careful." Sophia rushed forward, her disguise still in place, her cap hiding her hair, but her voice. It was unmistakable.

"Get the lady!" Lewiston yelled at someone swinging over the side of the ship from the wharf.

Bolider, damn it, and another man from the tavern too.

Donnelly had to get to Sophia. He ducked Lewiston's next blow then kicked the man's leg out from under him. Lewiston went down, hit his head on a crate and blood gushed, his eyes rolling until the whites showed, death taking him fast.

"Donnelly, behind you!" Sophia yelled.

More men swarmed on board, too many.

"I've got her." Bourbon nabbed Sophia around the waist and hoisted her up onto the upper deck by the wheel.

Donnelly barreled toward the new arrivals, Sawyer and Giovani hot on his heels.

The acrid scent of blood filled the air as more men fell to their swords.

"I didn't sign up for this." One man fled over the side of the ship, and a second joined him.

Donnelly charged, but let them go.

A scream pierced the night and he spun around.

Geoffrey struck his ribs and searing pain ricocheted through him. He staggered back from the brutal blow and patted his front and sides. No blood spilled. Hell, he must have caught the flat of the man's blade, and all due to Sophia's scream. He blew his woman a kiss, who thankfully remained safe, Bourbon guarding the stairs to the upper deck and slashing at those who came near.

Donnelly circled Geoffrey then ducked as he caught the glint of a flying dagger, a blade clearly meant for him. It whistled over his head and struck Geoffrey between the eyes. Geoffrey fell face-first into a crumpled heap against Captain Lewiston, while Bolider who'd tossed the dagger, swore under his breath.

Bolider stuck his fingers between his lips and an ear-piercing whistle shrilled. The remaining crew all turned tail and leaped over the side of the ship, Bolider stumbling drunkenly after them.

"Do we give chase?" Sawyer clasped the edge of the ship as he glanced back at him.

"No, enough blood has been shed here this night. Let them go." Bodies littered the deck, although thankfully not those of the men who'd fought at his side.

He met Sophia's gaze over Bourbon's and held out one hand. She scrambled down from the helm and raced across. Opening his arms, he caught his vixen, barely planting one foot back in time to stop them both from tumbling to the ground. "My sweet Sophia, you seem rather eager to see me."

"Are you hurt?" She patted him all over, her hands darting everywhere. "There's blood on your shirt."

"It's not mine, although my ribs took a beating from one brutal blow. Your warnings during the battle saved my life, which means I have one very wise seer to thank." He caught her face between his hands and with untold longing surging through him, kissed her long and hard. "From now on," he murmured raggedly against her lips, "I'm not letting you out of my sight."

"Oh my, that sounds perfect to me." She lifted onto her toes and inspected a scratch along his jaw then another on his neck. "You fought hard and so very well. You would have made an excellent hussar had you remained with your regiment."

"I hate to interrupt you both," Bourbon said as he joined them. "But we need to speak to Mr. Taylor, and preferably before he catches wind of what's happened here this night. I'll leave Giovani on board to ensure this vessel remains at berth since it needs to be searched for any of the missing items from within the chest. We'll take my coach."

"Agreed." Donnelly swept Sophia up and carried her to the side of the ship.

It was time to deal with Taylor, who would rot in hell for what he'd done.

Chapter 14

The coach rocked, and hooves pounded the street as Sophia sat next to James on the squabs, Anteros and Sawyer across from them. Never had she witnessed such a battle, but even as it had unfolded around her in all its viciousness, she'd rather have been there than anywhere else. James held her loyalty, as each of these men in this coach now surely did.

"How are you feeling?" James lifted her hand between both of his and gently kissed her chilled fingertips.

"Grateful for everyone here and worried about Giovani since we've left him behind. I'm also exceedingly angry that Mr. Taylor has gotten away with murder until this day." As they neared James's warehouse, the skies lightened, the dawn sun breaching the horizon and the ever-present morning fog thankfully lifting.

"Taylor's retribution is mere minutes away, and I can assure you he'll pay dearly for what he's done." He lifted her off the squab, settled her in his lap and wrapped his arms around her.

"James, what are you doing?" She squeaked and

wriggled to free herself. "Your actions are most improper," she whispered.

"You're calling my actions improper?" He grumbled under his breath as he glanced at the men across from them, both of whom continued to watch for their arrival at the docks, paying them no attention at all. "You're dressed in lad's clothing, have just witnessed a battle with blood being shed, and are shivering. I will hold you so I can warm you up, and nothing you can say will halt me."

Well, he had a point with all those arguments, and indeed, his heat penetrated deep into her, warming her in the most delicious way and settling her chills, not that she intended to admit that. Instead, she let out a low growl and touched the grim line of his lips. "You must confront your man of affairs soon. Are you ready to do so?"

"My father employed Taylor seven years ago, and I find it intolerable that he's been stealing from my family all these years." He removed her cap, set it beside him and smiled as her golden locks fell in soft waves around her face. He twined a lock around his finger, his strength fully enclosing her, his voice a husky murmur in her ear, "My lady, you have the most beautiful hair. It's so glorious in color, as stunning as the rising sun on a crisp spring morning."

"That sounded rather poetic." A side of James she quite liked.

"I want to see your glorious locks spread across my pillow every night." He touched his lips to her ear and discreetly ran his tongue along the whorls.

"Ah, t-that could be arranged." She gasped as something very large poked her in the bottom.

"You're willing to fill the position I've offered, of gracing my bed?" A spark in his hazel eyes, the color shifting from brown to a stunning green and oh my, how she'd missed seeing his eyes come so alive with such glorious color.

"The position sounds very tempting, although there must be a catch."

"You'd have to promise me your obedience," he added huskily.

"Obedience is a tad boring." She wriggled against him some more. "Stubbornness though...I can give you plenty of that."

A grimace as he reclined his head back against the coach seat.

"Do I have your agreement?" She wriggled some more.

"Sophia." A definite growl as leaned forward and nipped her ear. "My lady, I am presently suffering. In both heaven and hell."

"We've arrived," Bourbon stated.

The coach slowed and she craned her head to check out the window. Indeed, they'd arrived.

They drew up alongside another coach, the crest emblazoned upon it stating it belonged to the Duke of Ashten. She slid off Donnelly's lap, which thankfully he allowed, while outside Ashten's coach her brother-in-law stepped clear. With his cane in hand and navy tailcoats flapping, Ashten strode toward them with firm purpose.

The duke opened the door and stepped inside. Sitting next to Donnelly, he removed his hat and cast one slow and assessing look at her. "Olivia arrived on my doorstep a few hours ago in a fit of worry. She and Ellie have been fearing for you ever since. Are you well, Sophia?"

"Yes, and I'm sorry. I didn't mean to worry anyone with my sudden leaving, but I had no choice." She'd apologize profusely to Olivia and Ellie when she next saw them. "Are Winterly and Mama aware of my leaving?"

"No, thankfully not, although you'll have a devil of a time explaining all of this to your sisters, who I might add, insisted on traveling with me and are right now ensconced in my coach." He lobbed his gaze to Donnelly. "I thought it best to check here at your warehouse before continuing on to the eastern docks. Woodman said that's where you'd gone. What exactly has happened?"

Donnelly informed Ashten of Captain Lewiston's theft of the chest, of the captain's intention to set sail across the Atlantic and increase his wealth by means of pirating, and of their battle on board the captain's recently acquired ship. He spoke of Geoffrey Lewiston's involvement, then confirmed the demise of both brothers, and that they'd left Bourbon's man, Giovani, behind to take care of matters. Lastly, he updated him on Mr. Taylor, that Lewiston had confirmed his man of affairs had been pilfering cargo and squandering his family's money for years. Hands braced on his knees, James snarled, anger thrumming from him. "Ashten, I'm after a confession from Taylor, then I will ensure he pays for his crimes once I have the evidence I need for a conviction."

"He deserves death."

"Agreed, or to rot in Newgate, with no hope of ever seeing the light of day again. Either option suits me." James grasped her hand and gently rubbed it between his fingers.

"I apologize that this conversation is improper for you to hear."

"I need to hear it." Through good times and bad, she would stand by him.

"Taylor will be dealt with right now." A firm promise as he kissed her hand.

"We have visitors," Bourbon interrupted as he opened the door. "Wills approaches. Another lad too."

Indeed, two lads approached, both in breeches and dusty jerseys. They bounded in, grave looks in both their eyes.

"Speak, Wills," Bourbon ordered the boy with a mop of brown hair and soot smeared across one cheek.

"This is Paddy," Wills said with a wave of his grimy hand at the other boy.

"You're the cabin boy from the Fortune Maria?" Donnelly asked, and the lad named Paddy nodded. "Inform us of all you know."

"Milord, the first mate of the Fortune Maria asked me to find Captain Lewiston and I did, at the Boar Head Tavern. I snuck in through the back door near the kitchens and overheard the captain speaking to his brother. Geoffrey, his name was."

"What did you hear?"

"The owner said he had a buyer for his tavern, someone named Blackburne. The captain told his brother they'd be sailin' on the high tide, and to gather as many men as he could. I could tell Captain Lewiston was up to no good, but I wasn't sure who I could trust, so instead of going back to the first mate, I left and came straight here to find ye. Snuck a ride on a cart, I did, then asked Mr. Taylor if I could wait for ye in yer office. He asked me what I needed to see ye about, and I told him what I'd uncovered. He got mighty angry and backhanded me. When I woke up, I found myself in the basement of the warehouse." He gestured a shaking hand at Wills. "He got me out."

Wills cleared his throat. "Taylor is upstairs in the office where ye all spoke the other day. He's making a terrible racket, and he's got a pistol. I spied him with it."

"You two have both done very well." Donnelly glanced between the two boys. "These are your new orders. You're both to stay right here while we confront Taylor. You're to remain out of harm's way. Am I understood?"

"Yes, sir." Firm agreement and nods from the two lads.

"Good." Donnelly stepped down from the coach and held out his hand to her. "You're to wait with your sisters in Ashten's coach."

She didn't argue, but accepted his hand and once he steered her across to Ashten's conveyance and aided her inside, she got smothered by both her sisters and a dozen demanding questions.

Oh dear, she had a lot of explaining to do.

Chapter 15

Donnelly marched with Ashten and Bourbon along the docks toward his main warehouse that housed the offices, Sawyer having remained with the ladies to keep a guard. Vessels from Spain, Portugal, and Sicily were docked alongside English ships, the waters of the River Thames rippling as the new day began, a day when justice for his loved ones would finally be granted. He'd ensure it. Marching along, he strode past a cart overloaded with goods and a clerk with papers in hand, while a shout rang out as a driver rumbled along the cobbled street across from them.

Ashten pulled a pistol from his pocket, a murderous expression on his face, and Bourbon did the same, sliding his pistol free and stroking the barrel.

"I want a confession from him." He stayed Ashten and Bourbon's hands. "Although killers can get desperate, so by all means, remain on the alert."

With his own pistol in hand, he bounded up the warehouse stairs two at a time, shoved open the door of the main office and entered pitch blackness. Not even a spillage of light trickled through the window, the curtains pulled shut.

A click echoed. Sparks flared from a flintlock and—*boom.*

Donnelly dropped to the floor and rolled toward the wooden filing cabinet.

Boom, boom. A second and third shot blasted.

Smoke curled into the air from Ashten and Bourbon's pistols. Taylor grasped his belly, his weapon clattering to the floor.

"Sh-shot." Taylor tore the curtain from the rail as he floundered, his eyes rolling as blood poured from the two gaping wounds where his friends' shots had hit their mark.

He pocketed his pistol, which he hadn't yet fired, and caught Taylor as he crumpled. "Damn you. Why did you do it? Tell me, Taylor!"

"Your father knew about my squandering. He confronted me about his suspicions." A wheeze. "A-arsenic. I laced your father's brandy decanter. In his library following our meeting. He mustn't have drunken any until the next day. He came to the office sick and—he collapsed right here." A tap on the floor with his bloodied boot.

"What about my brother?" He wanted to put a shot in the man himself, but he forced himself to wait. To listen.

"S-same way. I added arsenic to his c-coffee when he came to look over the ledgers in the filing cabinet. I couldn't hide my thievery anymore." Blood trickled from his mouth, his head lolling. "Sh-should have disposed of their bodies another way, but I couldn't think c-clearly. Dumped them both in the river."

He choked, coughed, blood splattering everywhere.

Taylor's eyes slid shut and he slumped in his arms.

Donnelly dumped his body at his feet and wiped his hands clean of the man.

Bourbon hauled the torn curtain over Taylor and muttered under his breath, "Well, at least you got your confession."

"Yes, and for that I'm most grateful." He stroked his pocketed pistol, wishing he could fire it at the dead man.

Ashten poked a finger into the hole now gracing the office wall, right where Donnelly's head would have been if he'd not dropped so fast. "I don't believe we should speak of this near miss with the ladies," Ashten stated, quite firmly. "My wife is in a gentle state, expecting our first child."

"Agreed, and you have my congratulations." Donnelly clapped Ashten's shoulder, glad for the bright news in the middle of all the death and destruction. He turned and strode to the desk, his breath catching at the sight of a black leather-bound ledger. He'd never seen it before. Taylor had only ever presented him with burgundy leather-bound ledgers. He snagged it, then opened it under the light now streaming in through the window.

Taylor's notes were messy, several lines and amounts crossed out, along with notations on profits made on unrecorded sales. He thumbed through the entire ledger, every page the same. He'd clearly found the physical evidence he needed to prove Taylor's pilfering of his cargo.

He bowed his head.

His father and brother could now rest in peace, their killer no longer at large, and Taylor could never take the life of another of his loved ones.

Along with his friends, he'd ensured justice had been served.

Peace settled in his heart.

Chapter 16

Tightening the belt of her dressing robe, Sophia paced her bedchamber that evening. She clearly had little hope of seeing Donnelly again today, not now the hour was so exceedingly late. This morning, after he'd returned to the carriage with Ashten and Bourbon, the three men had informed them about Mr. Taylor's demise, although not the specific details. They hadn't wished to upset them.

It had been agreed that Ashten would see her and her sisters home, that he'd then speak to Winterly and Mama now the danger had passed and assure them all was well. Donnelly, meanwhile, had chosen to remain behind so he could converse with the Bow Street runner they'd sent for, and to liaise with the magistrate who would no doubt arrive soon, while Bourbon had taken his carriage to the eastern docks to join Giovani in uncovering what he could on board Lewiston's vessel.

Thankfully, Winterly hadn't questioned her any further on her involvement, and neither had Mama. They'd both accepted Ashten's word that everyone involved had now paid for their crimes, then hugged her tightly, their love washing over her.

"The night has turned quite cool. I'll have you warm in a moment, my lady." Abby stoked the fire.

A knock rattled the door and her maid dusted her hands on her white aproned skirts and opened it. She gestured the servants in. A maid entered with a tray and set it on her side table, while behind her two barefoot lads—the cook's sons—their brown breeches smeared with soot and their pale hair tousled, heaved a tub in and set it before the hearth. Along with her maid, they all left to fetch the water.

She seated herself, forked the salmon and took a bite. She usually adored salmon, but with her worry over Donnelly still strong, she couldn't taste it. Instead, she sipped her steaming tea and wished with all her heart that Donnelly was here, his arms wrapped around her.

At another knock, her maid returned along with the lads, each carrying steaming pails of water. They filled the tub and heat wafted through her chamber. Abby laid a bar of soap and a drying cloth beside her bath, then dipped her head and shut the door after her and the lads.

Hopefully a bath would relax her, allowing her to sleep for the night. She bolted the door and leaned back against the dark-grained wood. Burning logs crackled in the hearth, the light of the flames dancing across her red-gold bedcovers and the matching drapes pulled across her window.

She removed her robe and laid it over the chair closest to the tub then crouching, tested the water with a swirl of her fingers. Perfect.

Into the tub, she stepped then sank down, the water

gloriously warm as it washed over her. She dunked her head, staying under a little too long before surfacing with a gasp for breath.

"Good evening, my sweet."

She splashed water over the rim, hands slapping across her breasts. Donnelly stood inside her room, her drapes swaying and a whistle of cool air streaming through her now open window. "What are you doing here?"

"I realize the hour is incredibly late, that I shouldn't be visiting you in your bedchamber or while you are bathing, but you left your window unlatched and I couldn't help myself. I scaled the side of your house and snuck in. I assure you, no one saw me."

He closed her window, pulled the drapes shut and leaning one shoulder against the end of her four-poster bed, smiled rather charmingly. He'd changed clothes and now wore a sinfully dark pair of breeches and jacket, his cravat knotted and hair damp as if he'd recently bathed before coming to her.

"How did everything go?" She folded one leg primly over the other.

"All the evidence has been placed before the magistrate, including Taylor's admittance of murder and one very damning ledger that lists all of his swindling."

"What of Bourbon and Giovani? How did they fare at the eastern docks?"

"They found no sign of the chest, not on board the ship or at the tavern which now belongs to Blackburne, although Bourbon won't rest until he uncovers everything that was stolen from within it, no matter how long that might take, or what must be done. Bourbon and the magistrate also spoke to Blackburne at his solicitor's office. Another search was made of that premises, with nothing new uncovered. It appears Blackburne purchased the tavern with his own coin and had the legal paperwork on hand to prove his claim, and although we're not exactly certain of how deep Blackburne's involvement is in the scheme of things, we do know that he purchased the jade mask. Never fear though, Bourbon will keep a close eye on him."

"Thankfully, you've brought fairly good news."

"Yes, but hopefully the best news is still to come." He stalked closer, went down on one knee beside her, plucked her hands from her breasts and softly kissed her palms. "News of an impending elopement is what I speak of, and your agreement to run away with me, before this night is done." Another kiss, this time on her lips. "Lady Sophia Trentbury, I would be honored if you'd agree to be my wife. Will you marry me?"

"Oh my, I should warn you, that I can be a little willful."

"I would have you no other way."

"I also have a terrible habit of getting into trouble."

"We'll both work on keeping you out of trouble."

"Then yes." She grinned. "I would love to be your wife." Her heart overflowed with love, this moment one she'd been longing for. "You might need to pinch me, for I fear I'm dreaming."

"Pinching underway." He stroked the pebbled tips of her breasts, her nipples hardening, then smiling wickedly, he pinched them both. "I wish to bathe with you." A soft murmur.

"You appear as if you've already bathed."

"Two baths are better than one."

"I'm not sure there's any room in my tub for two."

"I'll find room, my willful love." Chuckling, he unlaced his boots and kicked them free before removing his black jacket and unknotting his cravat. He tossed his clothing onto the corner armchair, unbuttoned his shirt and standing before her in his breeches, flexed his muscles, his chest and biceps rippling in the dancing firelight.

"This will be a new experience. I've never bathed with a man before." Squirming back, she made more room for him.

"I should hope you haven't. I also intend on making this the most delicious bath you've ever experienced, with the promise of many more delicious baths to come." He gripped the waistband of his breeches where a tease of dark hair, the same color as his head, narrowed down his rigid belly and disappeared below the waistline.

She licked her lips and waited. "You are taking far too long to undress."

"Yes, I quite possibly am." He shoved his breeches down and exposed his thickly muscled thighs and an appendage that fully saluted her and marked him as a very virile man.

She stared at him, his cock growing even thicker and longer under her observant eye.

Stepping in, he sloshed the water and eased down. His gaze smoldered as he nabbed the soap and lathered it. Bubbles foamed everywhere, coating the surface of the water. "Say yes," he murmured.

"What am I saying yes to?"

"My touch, which will be everywhere that might

please you."

"Yes, most definitely yes."

"You're sounding rather biddable." He lifted one of her feet onto his shoulder.

"I shall endeavor to learn how to curtail my willfulness."

"Willfulness has its benefits, as you've now taught me." He stroked over her calf, teased across the sensitive skin behind her knee then smoothed along her inner thigh before pushing one finger deep inside her channel.

She barely bit back her squeal at his shocking move. She certainly slapped one hand over her mouth before she alerted the entire household to her current visitor. With her heartbeat racing, she whispered between her fingers, "You are all I've ever wanted."

"You're all I've ever wanted too. I also wish for you to lie back and relax. It's time to enjoy your bath." Grinning, he added a second finger and pushed in deep, touching a spot that had her arching her back. With his voice a sultry whisper, he murmured, "You're so beautiful, Sophia. I can hardly believe you'll soon be my wife."

"Keep touching me," she whispered in return.

"I want to do more than touch you. I want to devour you." He swished her hair from her breasts and caressed both mounds, his touch deliciously firm and tantalizingly sweet, his thumb tracing over her heart-shaped mole.

A fiery tingle radiated out from her sensitive nipples and she moaned.

"I need you closer." He clasped her bottom, lifted her out of the water and sat her astride his hips. Gently, he trailed kisses along her jaw and neck then moved lower and mouthed one breast. He sucked her nipple deep between his lips, pulling at first one and then the other.

"May I touch you in return?"

"Yes, wherever you please, particularly my cock. It's hungry to be gripped by you." He caught her hand and pushed her fingers under the water, wrapped them around his cock and guided her so she stroked him in long pulls. As she continued with the movement, he groaned in her ear, his cock getting harder.

"I like bringing you pleasure." She swiped her thumb over the plump head.

"I'll only ever find pleasure at your hand. I promise you, Sophia, only ever yours."

"James?" She nuzzled his neck, drew the soft skin deep into her mouth and sucked as she pumped him below.

"Too much," he groaned, his voice all hard and husky. "I'll never be able to hold on if you continue touching me like that."

"Isn't that what should happen, for you to come as you did the other night?"

"A man should be able to withhold from finding his own pleasure until he has well and truly sated his lady's. You can come again and again, not just once, as a man can."

"How wonderful."

"Would you like to see exactly how wonderful?" He lifted her hand from his cock and placed both her arms around his neck, then he shifted restlessly underneath her before dipping one finger through her curls and caressing her nub. "Move to your knees."

She lifted up a touch and he took his cock in hand,

then massaged the head back and forth over her nub until she wriggled and squirmed for more. "I adore having you so close."

"Remember, again and again." He pushed both fingers inside her and rubbed.

Tingles built into rapid bolts of pleasure that fired through her core, then she soared to the heavens and floated amongst a glorious array of stars.

Dreamily, she came back down to find herself being carried by James from the tub. He laid her on her bed and slid his body wetly over hers.

Taking her mouth in a ravenous kiss, every incredibly hard and defined inch of him gliding over her, she got lost again in such sweet pleasure.

Nothing separated them any longer, not his investigations, not his need to seek justice, not a world of death and darkness. No, he'd promised himself to her, and she'd promised herself to him.

Spreading her fingers through his damp locks, she allowed her instincts to take over and she pushed her hips toward his hips. "I wish for you to show me what it's like to join as one."

"I'm happy to wait until we've spoken vows. We could reach Gretna Green within the week and once we're man and wife, I promise you, there will be no holding back as I ravish you from that day on."

"I can't wait that long, not for a full joining. I want you deep inside me now. Willful, remember?"

"Are you certain?" He swept his thumb over her nub and sparks of pleasure pulsed through her.

"Yes, very certain."

"You intoxicate me."

"My heart is yours, James."

"I love you, Sophia." Kissing her, he stroked her harder and faster and she bucked, her pulse jumping out of rhythm and her desire and sheer need for him catapulting to the skies.

Chapter 17

Kissing and touching Sophia had James on the brink of no return. His cock throbbed for release, although he would see her come a second time before he took her innocence and drowned himself deep inside her. Her pleasure would always come first, each and every day from this day forth.

He slid down her body, tracing her skin with his mouth and tongue as he imbibed on her. He sucked madly on her full breasts, scraped his teeth over her pebbled nipples until she arched her back and whimpered for more.

After kissing her beautiful heart-shaped mole, right over her left breast, he teased his way down to her navel. He indulged himself on her creamy flesh, pushed her legs apart and lowered his head to her entrance. He wanted to know the taste of her, every single delicious inch.

Touching his tongue to her nub, he caught her shocked gaze as she elbowed up and watched him. She didn't halt him though. Thank heavens. He wrapped his mouth around her sensitive core and razzed the tip with his teeth.

This woman was his. She belonged to him, just as he belonged to her.

"Whatever you're doing, keep doing it." She gasped and clutched his shoulders. "It feels incredible."

"This is how I want to love you, to know your taste on my tongue, then to bury my cock here between these luscious pink folds." His mind went dark with lust and he nudged her legs wider and opened her up more fully for his touch.

"Have mercy." She collapsed back, her hand fisting against her mouth.

He drank her in and she convulsed, her core rippling under his lips.

No more waiting. He lifted up, moved between her legs and teased his cock along her wet folds. Claiming her mouth with his, he pushed against her thin barrier, tore through her innocence and plunged deep inside her.

"Oh, James." She sighed into his mouth, her fingers fluttering over his back. "You feel incredible inside of me, as if there isn't an inch of me not filled with you."

"Is there any pain?" He eased up, then slowly pushed back in.

"To begin with, yes, but the pain is already easing." She kissed him, and he slid slowly out of her then thrust deeply back in.

He pounded longer and harder, making her take all of him, every last inch and her inner walls hugged him, welcoming him.

"Don't ever leave me again, James." She clawed his back and his thoughts scrambled into a million pieces. He got lost, utterly and completely, her channel clamping down tightly on him and her inner muscles dragging him deep within her.

His release exploded violently from him, and she came right along with him, his seed shooting deep inside her. He rocked between her thighs until she'd taken every last drop he had to give, then breathing against her lips, he murmured, "My love, there is no one who can ever part us again. You belong to me, just as I belong to you."

It was time to sweep her away into his awaiting carriage.

Gretna Green their destination.

Her heart, his to always hold.

Chapter 18

A fortnight later, after returning from an elopement to Gretna Green where they spoke vows before an anvil priest, Sophia stretched out on James's bed at Donnelly House, the ornate blue and gold brocade curtaining surrounding his bed swaying in the morning breeze flowing through his partially open window.

At the end of the bed sat a settee with scrolled ends supported by sphinx heads on lion's legs, which was where James had made love to her when they'd first walked into his chamber late last night, the two of them not even making it to his bed in their dire need for each other.

They'd loved each other well this morning too, James awakening her as he slid into her body and took her swiftly to the heights of ecstasy. He stirred her desire now, plucking at her nipples and sucking the beaded tips deep inside his mouth. Insatiable man.

She sank her hands into his dark brown hair and reveled in the silky strands sliding between her fingers. "I do wonder what I ever did with my days before becoming your wife."

"You found a great deal of trouble, or do you need reminding?" A teasing smile as he sucked then released her nipple with a soft plop, the tip now a vibrant rosy red.

"That's right, I did." She guided his head to her other breast. "This one is missing out on your attention."

"An atrocity for certain." He sucked her other nipple deep between his lips, his cock stiffening and jabbing into her hip. A groan, his eyes sliding shut, his next words rumbling all husky and hard. "Do you like your new home?"

"Yes, very much." She smiled, butterflies taking flight within her middle. "You've yet to show me where my bedchamber is located. Is it close to yours?"

"We Donnelly men keep our wives in our beds and never allow them their own chamber."

"Well, since I have a deep attachment to both you and your bed, I believe that is a wise move."

"I crave you, Sophia." He swept his hands underneath her bottom and caressed her bare skin. "And I love every inch of you, from your sweet mouth to your exquisite mind."

"I love you too." She caught his face and covered his mouth with hers. Kissing him, a wild and frenzy need overtaking her, she climaxed without even his fingers upon her below. Pleasure rippled through her, wave after wave and she floated somewhere between heaven and earth. "James, come inside me."

"I'm on my way." He surged into her in one sure and strong thrust, then rolled his hips against hers in a timeless dance of love, one she couldn't survive without now he belonged to her. When his own release powered through him, his seed spurting free and coating her womb, she skimmed his wide shoulders and held on as she flew with him.

A little later, she stirred, her husband intimately kissing her neck.

His breath fanned her ear. "I forgot to show you my wooden box last night?"

"The one you collected from your study?" He'd done so after speaking about it, his eagerness to share its contents sparking her curiosity.

"Yes. Wait right here while I fetch it from the side table." He rolled out of bed, and she almost cried out at the loss of his weight on her.

Easing onto one elbow, she satisfied herself instead with the sight of his firm buttocks and long muscled legs on view. He strode across the room, then when he turned from the side table with the box in hand, she admired every inch of his shaft swaying between his legs. She flushed with heat at the carnal creature she'd become.

Grinning, he returned with the box, carefully settled it on the bed between them and handed her a key. "Open it, my vixen."

"Tell me what's in it." She fluffed her pillow behind her then rested her back firmly against the headboard.

"Since the first night we met, I've been writing you letters."

"You have?"

"Yes, and they're inside this box. My secret thoughts, now shared with you."

"Oh, James." She unlocked and lifted the lid. Hundreds of letters lay inside, and her heart squeezed in on itself. "You surprise me every day with how passionate and loving you are. I can't wait to read these letters."

"You can begin right now if you like. I'll entertain myself while you read." He lay down beside her, gently caressed her belly with swirling fingers. "The letter on the top is the latest one, which I wrote during our trip home from Gretna Green."

"This is beyond wonderful." She couldn't wait a moment longer. She broke the seal on the letter topping the pile, her fingers all jittery, then out loud, she read his letter,

"My dearest Sophia,
You're sleeping right now, your head on my shoulder, the carriage bumping along. My heart overflows with heavenly peace which you've brought me. When I hold you in my arms, my love for you grows stronger. You are an angel sent to me from my father and brother. I'm certain of it."

She sniffed, tears trailing down her cheeks.
"Keep reading." He kissed her tears away.

"My love, you have planted an ache within me, one of the very heart and soul, and I beg you for your promise, that you'll forever be mine, as I'll forever be yours.
Loving you endlessly,
James."

She set the box aside and holding his precious face in her hands, kissed him with sweet abandon. "Yes, I'll be yours, always and forever."

"I've never known such happiness as this." He lifted her up and holding her hips, eased her down over his hot, rigid length.

"To heavenly peace and all it entails," she whispered raggedly. May their love overflow their lives for all time to come.

She kissed the man who she'd never relinquish.

He was her new home.

JOANNE WADSWORTH

The Wartime Bride

~ COMING NEXT ~

Regency Brides Series, Book Three

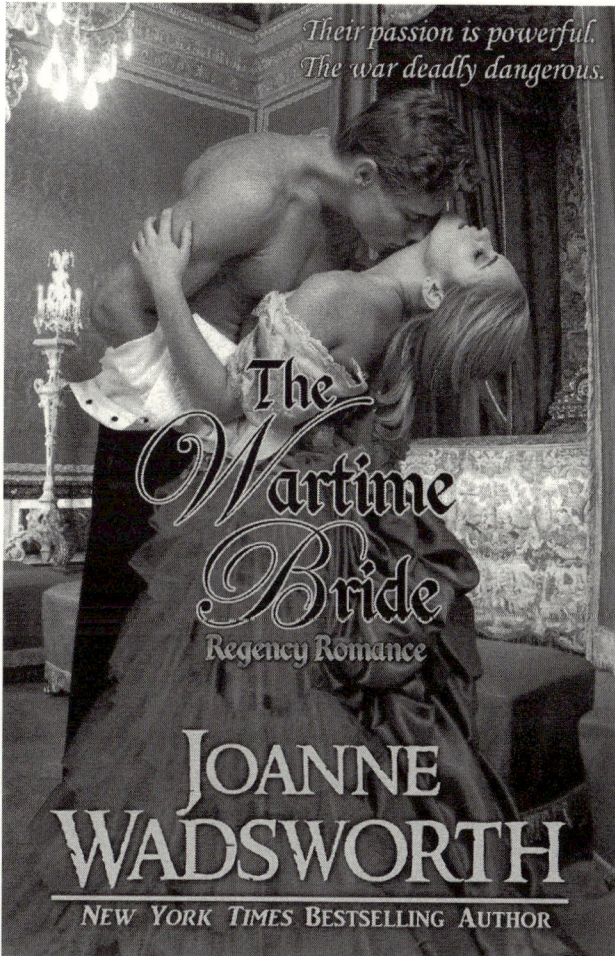

Regency Brides

The Duke's Bride, Book One
The Earl's Bride, Book Two
The Wartime Bride, Book Three
The Earl's Secret Bride, Book Four
The Prince's Bride, Book Five
Her Pirate Prince, Book Six
Chased by the Corsair, Book Seven

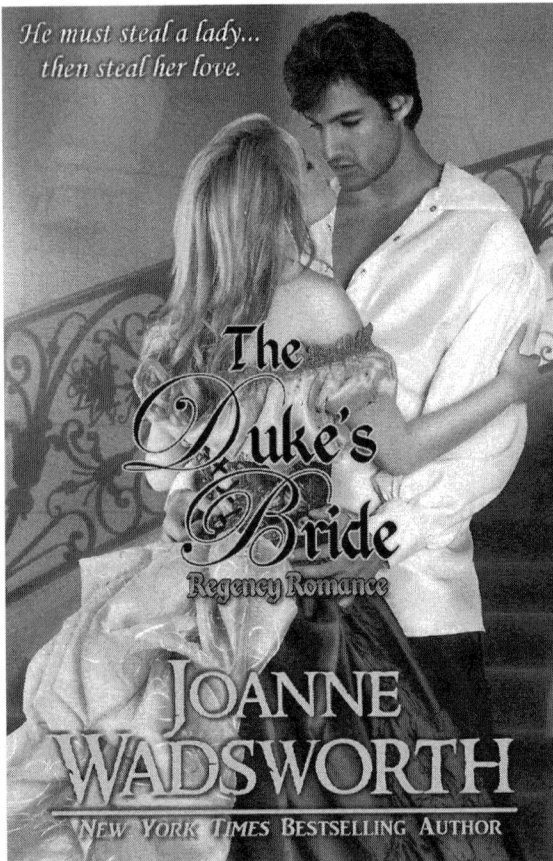

The Matheson Brothers

Highlander's Desire, Book One
Highlander's Passion, Book Two
Highlander's Seduction, Book Three

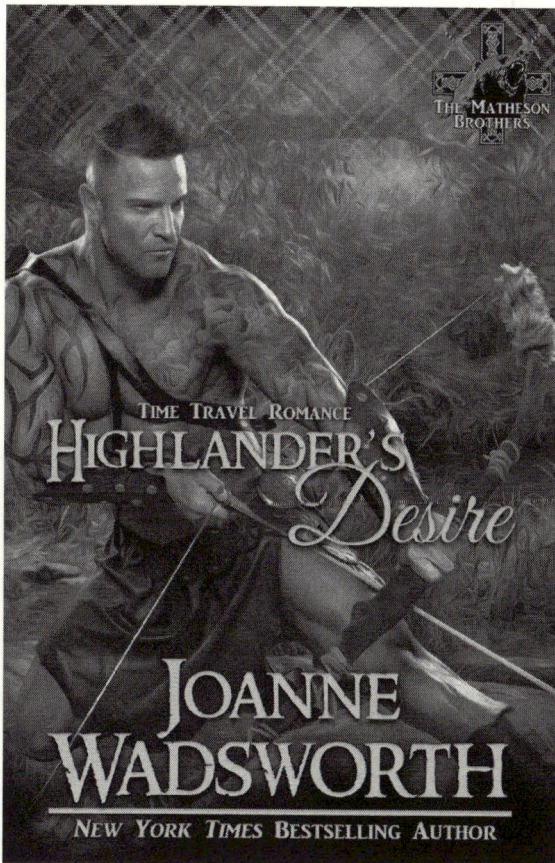

The Matheson Brothers Continued

Highlander's Kiss, Book Four
Highlander's Heart, Book Five
Highlander's Sword, Book Six

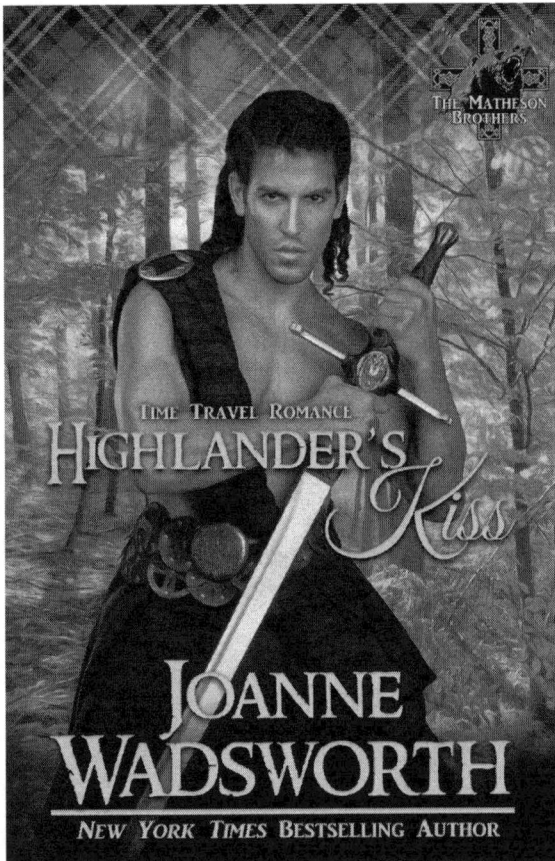

The Matheson Brothers Continued

Highlander's Bride, Book Seven
Highlander's Caress, Book Eight
Highlander's Touch, Book Nine

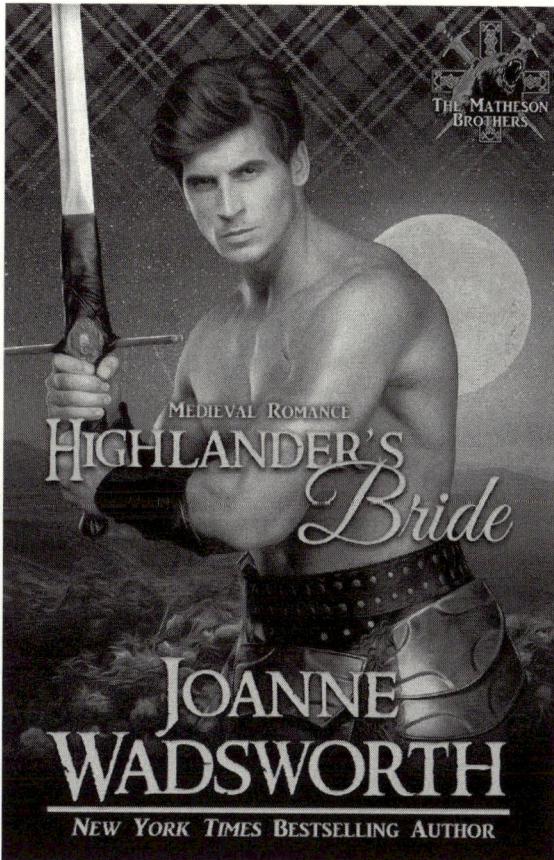

The Matheson Brothers Continued

Highlander's Shifter, Book Ten
Highlander's Claim, Book Eleven
Highlander's Courage, Book Twelve
Highlander's Mermaid, Book Thirteen

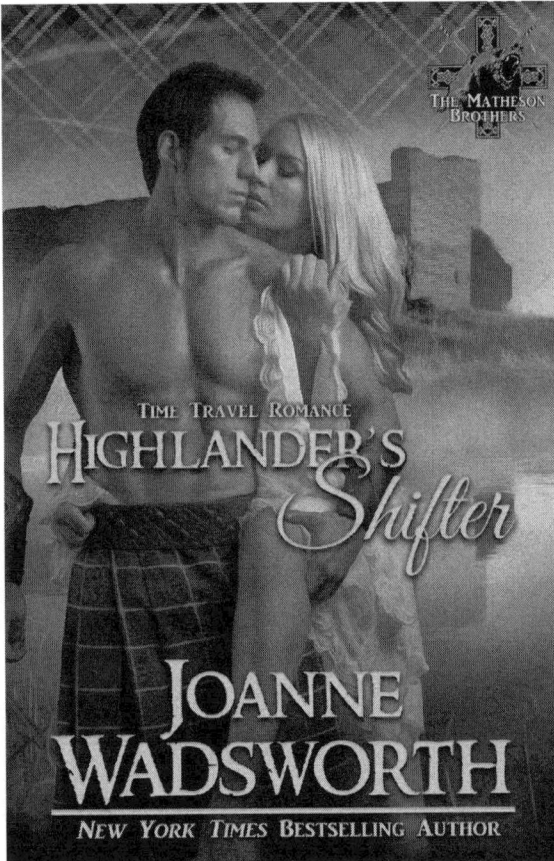

Highlander Heat

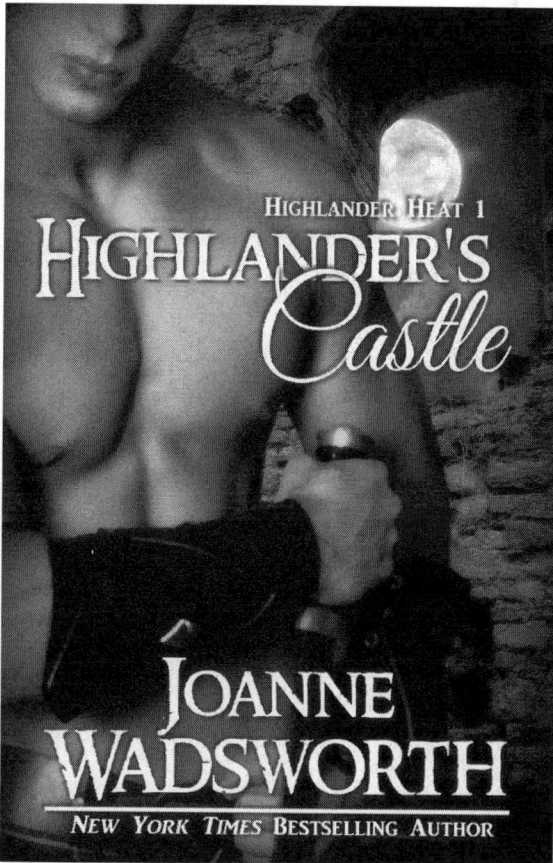

JOANNE WADSWORTH

Princesses of Myth

Billionaire Bodyguards

Billionaire Bodyguard Attraction, Book One
Billionaire Bodyguard Boss, Book Two
Billionaire Bodyguard Fling, Book Three

JOANNE WADSWORTH

Joanne Wadsworth is a *New York Times* and *USA Today* Bestselling Author who adores getting lost in the world of romance, no matter what era in time that might be. Hot alpha Highlanders hound her, demanding their stories are told and she's devoted to ensuring they meet their match, whether that be with a feisty lass from the present or far in the past.

Living on a tiny island at the bottom of the world, she calls New Zealand home. Big-dreamer, hoarder of chocolate, and addicted to juicy watermelons since the age of five, she chases after her four energetic children and has her own hunky hubby on the side.

So come and join in all the fun, because this kiwi girl promises to give you her "Hot-Highlander" oath, to bring you a heart-pounding, sexy adventure from the moment you turn the first page. This is where romance meets fantasy and adventure...

To learn more about Joanne and her works, visit
http://www.joannewadsworth.com

Made in the USA
Middletown, DE
06 November 2023